MW01702340

BRENTWOOD WOMEN MYSTERIES — BOOK 1

deliver us from evil . . . and the six o'clock news

W. H. ADAIR

Deliver Us from Evil . . . and the Six O'Clock News

Published by
Bungalow Books Publishing

ISBN: 979-8-9865364-3-9 (Paperback)
ISBN: 979-8-9865364-5-3 (Hardcover)
eISBN: 979-8-9865364-4-6 (eBook)

Copyediting and Proofreading by Kim Bookless
Cover and Interior Design by GKS Creative
Project Management by The Cadence Group

Library of Congress information on file with the Publisher.

This is a work of fiction. Names, characters, places, and incidents either are the product of the author's imagination or are used fictitiously. Any resemblance to actual persons, living or dead, events, or locales is entirely coincidental.

ALSO BY W. H. ADAIR

Deadly as a Walk in the Park (coming in spring 2024)
Murdered from Time to Time (coming in fall 2024)

WRITING AS WENDY H. ADAIR

The Broken Hallelujah

Winner of the 2023 Bronze Medal for wartime fiction
by the Independent Publishers Book Awards and finalist for the 2023
International Book Awards and the Page Turner Awards

WRITING AS WENDY ADAIR, WITH COAUTHOR OSCAR GUTIERREZ

Our Time: 75 Years of Learning and Leading

A history of the University of Houston

In memory of my sister Barbara Hilty Riley, who led the way with her romance novels, and my mother, Marjorie Hilty Gurasich, who carried the flag further, winning many awards for her YA historical works. You both continue to inspire me.

One

HILDY

Present

BRRRING.

Juggling my phone, the TV remote, and a pizza, I plopped down on the sofa, kicking off my sensible work heels. My left knee was still acting up weeks after the Costa Rica trip. I'd called Adrienne from the car and gotten her voice mail. No better luck now. She was supposed to meet me here to celebrate our great coup.

As head of PR for Gulf State University (Gulf U to insiders), I'd visited many places—Chicago, New York, London, even Lagos, Nigeria—while working with alumni, raising funds, and recruiting students. But digging in the dirt in Central America with eighteen- to twenty-year-old students was more fun than any of those fancier venues. I recently turned fifty, but no one would say Hildegard Brentwood couldn't keep up with the kids. We were nearly two miles above my normal sea level life, and my arthritic knee slowed me down, but thank God I remembered to bring the three-inch air mattress.

"With the latest update on the president's—"

Click.

I pushed the remote to get to the right channel. Shasta had already gotten in a face lick and pushed as close as possible to the pizza box. I tried again to reach Adrienne and got her *not here* message.

"The Rockets today—"

Click.

"—jungles of Central America, a group of Houston students uncovered mysteries centuries old. The Gulf State University students were led by their personal Indiana Jones, Dr. Adrienne Harrington. And our own Jack Tremayne was with them. Jack, tell us what you found."

I shivered at the mention of Jack Tremayne. He was one of the sleazy ones. Adrienne seemed leery of him at the dig. When I asked, she swore she'd met him once for dinner before the dig. He also seemed very familiar with Bobby Jake, Gulf U's golden boy quarterback and Adrienne's student assistant.

The screen filled with the posed helicopter shot of Tremayne arriving at the dig, and I laughed. They shot it twice to get it right. He was decked out in a green turtleneck under a hiking jacket with multiple pockets, khaki pants, and boots that gleamed in the morning light. An outfit straight from Indiana Jones. And of course he had the fedora, though he carried it . . . so it wouldn't mess his hair, I suspected.

The clip moved to the girl who discovered a silver spoon. Bobby smarted off that it was probably a bribe from the master to a woman he was "banging." Adrienne reined him in. Thankfully it wasn't said in front of Tremayne.

Shasta wiggled closer on the couch to get her tummy rubbed. The white schnauzer, whose name was shortened from *She Has To* (i.e., she has to be walked, she has to be fed, she has to sleep in my bed), stared at the pizza box without blinking—whoever blinked first lost, forfeited their piece of pizza. I think that was how she thought it worked.

"Well, Shasta, it's finally out."

We'd held releasing our story to coincide with the KRVU piece. It was the beginning of sweeps, three weeks after we returned from Costa Rica. This story had everything . . . smart female scientist, eager diverse students, and historical significance. The PR trifecta. It was about time they ran it. We posted the university's piece online that afternoon.

"Worth the week in the kennel, right?"

The doleful look should have made me grab a treat to appease the sad eyes. "No, I couldn't have left you with Minuit. You know Mother wouldn't deal with your craziness for a week. You might smudge something or bring in dirt. You aren't as refined as Minuit, but I adore you anyway. And I put you in the luxury dog suite at the Pet Hotel—it was painted with a Paris scene. I thought you'd love that." I refused to feel guilty.

My eyes were pulled back to the television. I locked back into my story and ruffled her ears. She didn't care about fame. Just food.

Shasta rolled back over to get another belly rub.

"Even if you didn't, I had a blast. OK, we worked in the sand and dirt all day with tiny brushes, but it was still fun . . . and where's Adrienne? She should be here celebrating with us."

Yes, I kept up a running commentary to a dog. Less crazy sounding than talking out loud to myself. I guess I could carry my cell and pretend to be talking on that . . . or get one of those fancy earpieces.

Picking up my phone, I checked for messages. Maybe Adrienne left a text. Nothing.

The story unfolded on the TV screen as I tried her number for the fourth time, listening all the way to the end this time so I could holler at her.

"Hi, you guessed it, I can't come to the phone, so leave a message at the beep, and I'll get back to you as soon as I can . . . *Beep*."

She should have been glued to her set at home if she wasn't coming over.

"Hmm, Ade. Hi, me again. Just wanted to call and gloat about our piece. It's great, and you and the kids look wonderful. Very scientific! Thought you were coming here. Hope you got a better offer and are out celebrating. Give me a call."

I turned my attention back to the screen, and the anchor moved on to the important happenings of the day . . . traffic wrecks, drug busts, shootings.

I was basking in my glory, even if I had to do it alone. Perhaps I should have invited Mother to my impromptu premier. Not sure she'd appreciate it. Although she would probably note the amount of work it took. That might strike a chord. *Oh well. Don't really need an audience. I'll get my accolades at work.*

I was about to chow down on the cold pizza when my cell rang with the Gulf U fight song. As I reached for it, a *Breaking News Bulletin* flashed on the screen. The cameras were on campus.

Staring at the screen, I automatically answered "Hello" into the cell.

It took a few moments to sort out the stereo sounds—the reporter on the television screen and the voice on the phone.

"Ms. Brentwood, is that you?" a familiar voice asked.

Still trying to catch what was being said on the screen, I mumbled something.

The television was saying at the same time, "Just in from Houston Police, this late breaking story of tragedy on the Gulf State University campus . . ."

Great, just what we need, some drive-by shooting on Fraternity Row. It will totally erase all the good vibes from Adrienne's story.

The voice on the phone was still trying to get through. "Ms. Brentwood, Hildy, this is Charles West. We've got a situation, and we're going to need you to handle the press."

My shoulders dropped back down from around my ears. *Good, the chief of Gulf U police. He'll know what's going on.*

But it was the visual message that got through first. As Chief West continued speaking, my eyes were glued to KRVU's ubiquitous investigative reporter Jack Tremayne. He stood in front of the social sciences building, police car lights flashing in the background.

"Well, Sherry, this tragedy tonight sure provides an eerie coincidence for us at KRVU. We just aired our exclusive report on Dr. Adrienne Harrington's archeological work in Costa Rica, and we are now at Gulf State University reporting on what appears to be a double tragedy."

"Oh my God," I gasped into the phone, while staring in disbelief at the screen.

"According to our exclusive police sources, Dr. Harrington, and we believe one of the students we just saw on our exclusive video, were found dead in this building. Gulf U and Houston police authorities won't elaborate at this time, but we'll stay with this one. Back to you, Sherry."

"Ms. Brentwood!" Chief West's voice was getting edgy, even for a twenty-five-year police veteran and former LAPD detective.

"Oh, sorry. Yes, Chief, I'm here. Is it true, what I just heard that slimeball Jack Tremayne at Channel 7 say? Is Adrienne Harrington dead?"

I still couldn't pull my eyes from the TV.

"That's what I just said, Hildy." The Gulf U Police Chief answered, more patiently than I expected.

"We need you over here now. Channel 7's already on site, and I know the rest of the vultures will follow fast."

"Of course. I'll be there as soon as I can."

Moving as a trained public relations automaton, I stood up, not even looking down to avoid tripping over Shasta. Luckily I hadn't shed my work attire. My heels had ended up under the couch, so I slipped into more comfortable shoes, put the pizza on top of the counter, and whistled the dog to the back door. *She'll be fine in the yard for a few hours,* I thought, dropping a chew toy on the deck to keep her amused.

Grabbing my purse, I automatically locked the door and headed for the car. The damn phone jangled in my pocket. The theme from *Maleficent* rang out. I hit the red button. If I stopped to talk to Mother now, I'd never get to campus. After rejecting the call, I texted her. *Busy now. Call in am. All OK.* I figured the call was about the tragedy and not my video piece. She could hold until morning.

Throwing the car into drive, I headed to Memorial Park. The crush of drivers exiting downtown for the more refined suburbs had dropped to a trickle, and the scenic drive was much safer than the freeway in my frazzled state. I expected to be hit hard as the reality set in, but for now I felt nothing . . . numb all over.

If I'm lucky, the numbness will last for the next few hours. If I'm very lucky, I'll make it through the night before it becomes real.

Two

ADRIENNE

One Month before the Dig

ADRIENNE HAD LESS THAN a month before wrangling a dozen students and now a damn news crew to Costa Rica. No way she could pull everything together in time. At least she'd filed her grades for the semester. One thing off her list.

Greatest benefit from the winter break is not dealing with Gruesome Gus until after Martin Luther King Jr.'s birthday, she thought, taking a moment to savor it. She was giving her boss until the start of the next term to move on her tenure approval. Otherwise she was bringing in her lawyer and throwing her contract on the dean's desk with the papers for a discrimination suit.

She shook off the negative thoughts and looked over the materials she needed for the dig. She pulled out thumb drives with the basics of the surveying grid system and the methodology for gently uncovering possible specimens. Each student would get a kit with brushes, a small hand pick, a trowel, safety glasses, a line and surface level, a knife, and five hundred feet of surface line. Twelve kits plus one for Hildy and at least one for the KRVU reporter. She'd put together fifteen just in case. The students would probably keep their notes in their phones, but she had the proper small notebooks for each of them as well.

One more look around the office to make sure everything was in order. She took a second to admire how she'd made the small space her own, filled with books and mementos from her many journeys. In the box on her desk, she thumbed through the waivers for any injuries incurred—per the lawyers—medical kit, her own personal kit, and maps of the area. Approvals and government authorizations. Check and check. Still time for any last-minute changes and to verify travel arrangements. A dozen students for four days in the jungles of Costa Rica with Hildy, the videographer, and a local guide the only adults. She shook her head, wondering if she were a raging idiot.

At least her student assistant, Bobby, could help keep the others in line. *He's a real surprise for a football player.* Adrienne figured he counted on this course being an easy elective for his political science degree. Turned out he had a real aptitude for the work and earned his internship and more.

If she hurried, she might escape the office unnoticed. The harsh ring of the office phone broke through the divine silence of the post-fall graduation and pre-spring term emptiness of the faculty offices. As if on cue, there he was, Gruesome Gus Minor, chairman of the department and her personal nemesis. *How the hell does he know I'm here? Ah, hell. No escape. He'll see me passing his office on the way out.*

"Professor Harrington here."

A harrumph and gravely cough preceded the response. "Ah, yes, Dr. Harrington. See me before you leave for the holiday. I'm in my office now."

She'd skipped makeup on her day off. Not that she cared what Gus Minor thought of her appearance. But he'd add it to his list. At least she'd put on a bra before coming to campus.

"Male faculty never have appearance checks for dried food on ties, or sandals with socks," she mumbled. She did smooth her dark hair back into a ponytail. Her torn jeans, frayed Gulf U sweatshirt, and GORE-TEX boots would have to suffice.

Grabbing her satchel, she pulled the door closed. The department chair's office was in the corner of the building, overlooking the fifteen-foot statue of Rutherford Masterson. The founding dean and trust fund heir had donated $10 million for a scholarship endowment. Adrienne imagined Minor cursed him every morning for not leaving the money for administrative support.

Sauntering into his fiefdom, she paused at the door before entering.

"Yes, yes. Don't dawdle. Come in. Sit there." Dr. Minor spoke in cutoff phrases as if he were too important to build complex sentences.

His office screamed of his position. Diplomas and certificates were framed in gold. He was shaking hands with some VIP in every photo. No family pics. No shots of a dog or cat or ferret. No potted plant but a number of copies of the book he authored on his own tenure trail. He was seated behind an antique desk topped with deep brown leather . . . not university-issue.

"Harrington. You are taking responsibility for a number of students."

He glared at her, his eyebrows seeming to move independently on his square, craggy face.

"Sir. You mean my university-authorized dig and field trip?"

Minor dropped his gaze, staring at a stack of papers in the center of his desk. "Exactly. Your actions reflect on this department.

The university and college. I'm watching you. You will keep your students in line. And yourself in order."

She took three deep breaths. "Dr. Minor. These are young adults who have signed insurance waivers. This is not my first dig with students in the field. I do not need babysitting."

As much as she tried to control it, the words tumbled out.

He smirked like he'd won a point. "Harrington, you are an associate professor. Your tenure application is under review. I'll exercise my responsibility as I see fit."

Three deep breaths were not enough. Adrienne bit her cheek to keep from screaming.

"You're holding up my tenure review from going to the dean and provost. Let me remind you, *Doctor* Minor, I had tenure at University of Virginia. I came here with a promise and an appointment letter stating that my application for tenure would be reviewed within one year—which was more than two years ago. My materials have been filed for eighteen months. I'm not going to wait much longer before lodging a formal breach of contract and discrimination complaint. And from what I've heard, it won't be the first time you've been charged."

He slipped into a glare as she continued.

"If my tenure application doesn't move forward by the start of next term, my lawyer and I will be speaking with the dean and the provost. Tenure might protect you from being canned, but they can still remove you from your administrative duties and this fancy office."

She wanted more than anything to slam the door as she left, but she grabbed the handle and gently pulled it until she heard the click.

Three

HILDY

Present

CHARLES WEST WAS WAITING in the campus parking lot. There'd been violence on campus before, a few thefts and a very messy explosion in the chemistry lab that badly burned a grad student last year. In those cases, it wasn't that difficult to maintain the necessary journalistic detachment.

But murder, murder involving a friend, was something nobody was trained for.

Chief West, on the other hand, had been to many murder scenes in his previous life as an LA homicide detective. Thankfully, he met me at the car, opening my door as I sat there mesmerized by the flashing red and blue lights.

"Hildy. Hildy, come on. We need you out here." He pulled my arm until my body slid out of the front seat. He held on as he reached in, pulled the keys from the ignition, and pushed the automatic door lock button. Maneuvering my unresponsive body from behind the door, he closed it with a bang.

I jumped at the noise, my eyes finally refocusing. I was surprised to already be at the campus. I looked down at my dark blue slacks and blazer, the striped blouse. OK, fully dressed. Hopefully no one would look down at the old cordovan loafers I'd grabbed instead of work heels. They probably needed to go to Goodwill after this.

"Chief." I was proud that my verbal skills were still there, but I needed to do better if I was going to be much help. "Uh, my autopilot must have brought me to campus. I don't remember one intersection, red light, or traffic merge." Damn, my voice quivered.

"You all right now?" he asked, more gruffly this time now that I was verbal.

My fingers automatically dragged through my short red-gray hair, a usual response to stress. "Uh, yeah, sure, I guess so."

The chief's hard-nosed visage was back tightly in place. "OK, let me show you what we've got here. Then to the room where we've stashed all the hyenas."

He used his bulk like he was herding cattle, pushing and ramming through the throng of curious students, neighbors, strangers. At five foot four, I barely came to his shoulder, so I just traveled in his wake to get through. The crowd appeared from nowhere, like piranha, their cell phones snapping away in a vicarious feeding frenzy.

The crowd stared as we pushed through. For all they knew, I was the prime suspect. At least someone important. After all, I was getting to go in, and they weren't.

Once beyond the curious, we ducked under the yellow police crime scene tape. I gave a slight nod and a weak smile as we passed between two officers I usually encountered doing crowd control for rock concerts. They barely acknowledged our presence, staring straight ahead, solemn as the guards at Buckingham Palace.

Out in front were both Gulf U and Houston cop cars. Usually the jurisdiction was clear-cut. Campus police were licensed state peace officers, overseeing the safety of persons and property of the state, not the city. They cooperated, of course, but the Houston police had more than enough to keep them busy, so they left these particular five hundred acres of state land in the hands of Chief West. Even in the case of violent action, it was very unusual that the city boys in blue were already on the scene.

I could see West wasn't happy with the situation. His jaw tightened when he had to pull his badge to show the young HPD officer at the front of Masterson Hall.

I tried to focus my fractured concentration on the interesting political implications of the joint investigation. Chief West moved us into the building where even more officers stood guard. Taking the elevator to the seventh floor, we walked down the hall to the tape-covered door. Lights were flashing in the small office, reflecting off the walls and windows like a professional photo shoot. My eyes scrunched nearly closed as I tried to focus on anything but the two bodies.

Blood was pooling on the Persian rug covering most of Adrienne's office, turning the soft green and ivory almost black. It filled my vision, reddish-brown seeping out from under the white shrouds covering two bodies. It imposed itself on everything in my world. I closed my eyes and reached out to Chief West's arm to stay upright.

I was locked in place, and West gently tucked my arm into his and guided us a few feet from the scene to make room for the morgue attendants. They lifted the bodies onto stretchers, transferring them into large, dark cocoons with zippers—*body bags*, they called them in the movies.

Finally I succumbed to primal curiosity and stared at what was once a close and good friend. There was no way the shrouded being on the gurney could really be Adrienne. Adrienne was vibrant and funny, not cold and still. This was some dreadful mistake.

I held that fantasy close to get through the rest of the night, chanting in the back of my mind a personal mantra, *It's only a dream. I'll wake up and have a real laugh with good old Adrienne on this one.* Self-delusion is a very useful management tool.

"Sorry, Chief. I know I'm not being much help." I was in better control after the morgue attendants pushed the gurneys into the elevator and out of sight. "Tell me what we can release, what I need to check out for you, and where you've stashed the honorable gentlemen and ladies of the fourth estate."

He dropped my elbow and stepped a few feet away. "Good, I'm glad you're with us. We only have Channel 7 and 12 here now, but we're hearing from all the others, and even some from out of town. And, of course, we have a slew of young internet bozos who've wrangled press credentials from the city and gotten a free pass into the action."

Running his large paw of a hand across the top of his head, he barely disturbed his gray hair, cut military short. "We don't have much we can say, really, which I know makes your life harder."

We'd worked together on release of police information for years and had come to an understanding of the difficulties of our different jobs.

He laid out the specifics. "Dr. Harrington and a young man, who we believe was a student of hers, were found by the custodian at approximately 6:15 tonight. She was starting her nightly sweep through the building. She found the office unlocked and nearly tripped over them." His mouth tightened before he continued. "The woman recognized Dr. Harrington immediately and called us at 6:18 p.m., according to our logs. Our dispatcher used

Dr. Harrington's name when she sent out the call. That's how it got on the air so damn fast on Channel 7. They monitor all our police calls, same as HPD."

He frowned again as he mentioned the breach of protocol. Pity the poor rookie dispatcher. She was in for a real reaming tomorrow.

"Anyway, our guys got here by 6:22 and found essentially what you just saw—the bodies haven't been disturbed. They were both lying in front of her desk, the woman fallen forward and the boy on his back in quite a lot of blood."

He watched closely as he recited the details, shifting into the impersonal references no doubt to make it easier to stay detached, as I took notes for the upcoming briefing.

He was now getting into details that would hopefully never be released to the general public. "When we finally moved the woman's body, she was laying on some sort of long knife or dagger. We'll have to test it, of course, but it appears to be the murder weapon. Her hands were wrapped around the hilt."

He touched my arm as he continued, again offering moral support or something.

"The boy had stab wounds in his chest and shoulder. The coroner will confirm, but it appears the one to his chest was the fatal one."

His voice seemed to fade out until his hand tightened on my arm, bringing me back.

"Here, do you need a glass of water or something?"

From the look on his face, mine must have turned gray. "No, I couldn't." I gulped back the sour taste in my throat. "No, I'm OK, just give me a second. Do you know who the boy is . . . was? And tell me again, just what of this is public? What can I tell these guys?"

Chief West looked relieved I was back in business mode. "Well, really very little. We found some ID on the kid and have tentatively identified him as Robert Jake Jr., Dr. Harrington's student assistant. No formal ID has occurred for either victim. We can't release his name until we've notified his family. They have Dr. Harrington's name, but we can't officially confirm it for the same reason."

I didn't really know Bobby Jake, except seeing him on the dig and, of course, on the football field. But Adrienne and I became friends shortly after she joined the faculty nearly three years before.

"I don't think she had any . . . family, that is. None in the area anyway." I hardly recognized my strange monotone voice.

Looking over at me, West held a beat before continuing. "Well, we'll wait anyway until we can confirm that. You can give the broad sketch of what is official. That is the time the bodies were reported and that we are investigating it as wrongful deaths. And then, of course, your usual administrative response."

Yeah, the usual . . . President Murphy is horrified, blah, blah, blah.

"What if I get asked about who is conducting this investigation?" I shut my notebook, looking at the chief, ready to face the really tough job.

Chief West's face went from grim to gruesome.

"Whatever crime has occurred, it took place on state property. It, therefore, will be investigated by the university police department, in full cooperation with all other investigative authorities in the area who might be able to provide critical assistance." His demeanor brooked no response, so I straightened up, ready for an escort to the media holding pen.

The chief's stubborn adherence to strict jurisdictional protocol would be fine, if they cleared it up in a few days. The university would risk accusations of administrative cover-up if it took longer. My boss, Max, and President Murphy would be sure to weigh in on that point later.

I straightened my shoulders outside the conference room in the library across the quad. Twenty reporters and technicians were setting up to dissect my friend and a young man who could never defend themselves no matter how horrible the lies or innuendos. KRVU's team was conferring in the corner. They had the advantage of video from the dig, including their reporter on the scene. Tremayne was checking his tie in the polished steel of the light bar. The internet diva standing next to him popped gum as she scrolled through her phone. The Telemundo crew was checking with their editor for the countdown to go live.

I knew most of these reporters, even the kids on their phone recorders. Jack Tremayne was senior. He was practicing his broadcast smile, which never quite made it to his eyes.

Flipping on the mike, I tapped the top and waited ten seconds. "Quiet, everyone. Chief West has a brief update on the investigation. This will be short, so he won't be taking questions."

As Chief West walked into the room, there was a moment of absolute silence that erupted into a screaming match to see who could get recognized first.

"Chief, Chief. Can you tell us what's happened? Who was the kid? A student? Was this a lover's quarrel?"

The questions were coming all at once. It was nearly impossible to tell who was asking what.

Tremayne's strident tones took command of the room. "Chief, can you confirm that the student murdered was Bobby Jake, son of state senator Robert Jake?"

My jaw dropped, and I quickly pulled on my game face. How did Tremayne know his identity? Bobby Jake was not only the son of a state senator but he was also Gulf U's shining example of the successful student athlete—captain and quarterback of the football team, honors student in political science, and possible student body president next year. He'd been a focus of the video shoot in Costa Rica. The perfect example of the complete student. Senator Jake might explain the obtrusive HPD presence.

Chief West's face remained a complete cipher. He showed no surprise at the question. He glared at the reporters, waiting for some semblance of order. My cue.

"All right, folks, back off. We won't begin until there's quiet." I was amazed at how in control I sounded. "Chief West has some basics he can give you, but we are not in a position to release names of anyone at this time. You know that the families must be notified and formal identification must take place."

"But it was Dr. Harrington, wasn't it, Hildy?" The question came from Sandy Quinn, reporter for the *Chronicle*.

I took a deep breath to center myself before answering. "Sorry, Sandy, no official confirmation of that is possible yet."

Bless the laws regulating release of information. Sometimes it was easier when the law prevented talking—less of a tightrope to walk between the public's right to know and protection of an individual's privacy. It was especially welcome now, when I really didn't want to go over gory details of my friend's death.

"OK, then." Tremayne's voice pushed through again. "Let's get this official bullshit over with. What laundered shreds of information can you graciously impart?"

Ignoring him, Chief West briefed the group, telling them he had only ten minutes. In a monotone trained by years of talking to grieving relatives, he delivered the bare bones, turning an incident of high emotion, passion, and energy into a cold litany of stage direction and photographic reportage.

"The two victims are a white female, approximately thirty-five to forty years of age, and a Black male, approximately twenty years old. Both apparently died of stab wounds, possibly inflicted by a weapon found at the scene. The coroner will have to confirm that. Death is believed to have occurred after 3:00 and before 6:00 tonight. Again, that will hopefully be narrowed following the coroner's examination."

I refused to think about what such an examination might entail.

"We are proceeding with our investigation. Anyone who might have information or have seen anything suspicious on campus this afternoon should immediately get in touch with campus police."

"I heard HPD thinks this is a murder-suicide." Tremayne almost sniffed the air in anticipation. "Was this some illicit faculty-student tryst, perhaps reverse sexual harassment turned sour?"

"That's enough!" I barely kept from shouting, my voice sounding harsh even to me. After all, I should be used to these guys asking tough, cruel questions.

"Chief West must get on with his responsibilities here. We'll keep you apprised of developments as they are verified. I want to officially point out that Gulf State University has an exemplary record of safety for our students and employees. This is the first violent death on campus in over ten years."

I dropped back into boilerplate, and my voice took on an official drone.

"The president and the campus are horrified at these deaths. Provost Bryant is assigning counselors to be available to the campus community. And President Murphy has instructed Chief West to pull out all stops, working with area investigative units to solve this case and put the concerns of our students, faculty, staff, and our community to rest."

As soon as West quit talking, and while I gave the usual university response, the crews packed up to get the last shots of bodies being put in hearses and police crime scene specialists scurrying about their duties. They had all heard my obligatory speech in some form in the past.

West slipped out quickly, moving silently through the snaking cables.

I was left hanging on to the edge of the podium to get control. Tremayne sidled over. I shuddered as he touched my arm much too possessively.

"Come on, Hildy. We're friends, right?" He grinned, sharklike. "We were both down in the jungles with those two. They were lovers, weren't they? I thought I caught a glimpse of something when I was filming. You know I protect my sources. The powers that be will never know where I got it."

Wrenching away from his grasp, I replied softly, ice dripping from each word. "You have permission to leave. There is nothing I can tell you, and I assure you that there is nothing I will tell you."

My voice was steady. I spoke slowly, shaking inside yet somehow glad for the diversion. The slimy question forced me to concentrate on him and the job rather than on Adrienne and the confused and horrific images that kept swirling through my mind.

Tremayne laughed, slipping his slim notebook back into his jacket pocket. "That's OK, old girl. I understand. I can do this the hard way, too, you know." He turned on his heel and sauntered from the room.

Four

WALKING SLOWLY FROM THE briefing room, I focused on home. I would be there in less than thirty minutes and could lock myself away in a steaming hot bath. My stomach couldn't handle food, but a large glass of wine was in order.

Chief West had another idea. "I'm sorry, Hildy. We need one other favor."

Looking around, I didn't spot any stragglers from the media. Before I could ask, he pushed forward.

"We checked the records, and it looks like you're right. Dr. Harrington doesn't have any family listed on her paperwork, at least no one local. We need someone to make the official identification. Someone who knew her well and can swear to her identity."

His eyes stared at the ground. Mine grew huge. "Me? Jeez, I can't do that." Now my stomach started calisthenics.

"Please. I know this is hard, but we have to have an official signature." His hand on my shoulder held me in place, preventing my flight mechanism from kicking into gear. "I suppose we could call Dean Garner, but he wasn't close to her. And you know he'd really freak out. If not you, what about Chairman Minor?"

"Oh God, no. They hated each other. Adrienne would die if he were to see her that way." I shrugged my shoulders at the awkward *die* note.

"So it looks like you're the best. I'll send Sgt. Morris with you, and then he'll take you home. We'll get your car home while you're at the morgue."

Shivering, I fell back on sarcasm. "Anything else I can do for you guys? Sweep the rug for microscopic threads?"

My smart mouth was lost on the chief. As I babbled away, Sgt. Morris picked up my bag, handing the keys to West. He took my arm and led me inexorably to his squad car. I was still rattling on as he closed the door on my tirade.

My body shrank into the seat, folded into the fetal position. *I need to work on saying no.*

The ten-minute trip to the medical center seemed to take no time . . . and forever.

I'm a professional. I can do this, kept running through my brain in a continuous loop.

Sgt. Morris pulled into the loading dock. Again, someone was pulling my reluctant body from an automobile. Hopefully not a trend. Holding on to my elbow, neither of us spoke as he pushed the double doors open, letting out frigid air. I was already shivering, more from the idea of what was just down the hall than the sixty-degree temp. We faced a long corridor with gray and black linoleum on the floor and pale green walls. At the end of the hall were double doors with a code lock requiring an ID swipe.

The sergeant passed his card through the reader, and the doors swung inward. The temperature seemed to drop another ten degrees. Ahead were three metal tables; two of them held shrouded bodies. The coroner stood beside the first table, waiting. I couldn't look at the sheet, so my eyes wandered around the room. It was almost as pristine as NCIS led one to believe. Stainless-steel drawers lined the walls like huge filing cabinets filing the remains of a life, as unrevealing as paper files in defining who and what a person was.

Each table had a set of lights overhead like an operating room. The strong white lights leeched out all color. It was like a white-out blizzard, broken only by the stainless-steel tables.

The smell wasn't surprising. Formaldehyde, alcohol, bleach. It coated the back of my throat, astringent, bitter. The cold was boring into my bones, and my knee ached.

I'll need to up the glucosamine tonight.

I was in a bubble. If the machines had a hum and the fluorescent lights had an electric buzz, I didn't hear any of it. Finally I forced myself to look at the man standing next to the white-sheeted figure. I'd be damned if I'd throw up in front of the coroner.

The sergeant stood behind us, inching me closer to the table, no doubt ready in case I keeled over. It was so hard to look at Adrienne, and even harder to look away. Staring, unblinking, even unfeeling, I was as rigid as the corpse. The coroner lifted the edge of the sheet, turning back the corner to just under her chin.

Adrienne's beautiful face and bare shoulder lay there uncovered, vulnerable. The tan she'd been so proud of when we returned from Costa Rica was ashen gray. Her dark hair, which she always wore in a ponytail, hung loose, making her look even more defenseless.

I probably would have stood there staring for hours except the coroner coughed, and then Sgt. Morris spoke in his official voice.

"Ms. Brentwood, can you identify this woman as Dr. Adrienne Kimball Harrington?"

I nodded.

"Can you please say it for the record?" he asked.

"Yes." My voice cracked. Turning to Sergeant Morris, I asked, "Can you give me a minute? Just a few moments with her?"

They stepped back. I reached out with just a finger, not quite touching the cold shoulder. Whispering more to myself than to Adrienne, I made a vow. "The wolves are howling already, my friend. Some are saying you killed Bobby and yourself. I know you couldn't have done that."

Finally, I nodded, and kept nodding until Morris stepped up and pulled me back. I couldn't tell whether he'd heard my promise to Adrienne, but it didn't matter. The coroner moved the sheet back in place, turning Adrienne into an anonymous statistic, the twelfth violent death in Houston for the new year.

Shuddering, I walked from the room. Nausea was turning to anger. Adrienne was not a murderer. She did not do this. The media had it wrong. Possibly even the police.

I won't stand by and see her labeled a murderer.

It was after midnight when the sergeant dropped me home. I barely reached the couch before dropping my bag and kicking off my shoes. Sinking into the sofa, I tried to keep the bile from rising as I relived the sight and smell of the blood in Adrienne's office and the scent of death in the morgue.

I would keep my promise and find answers and justice for her. No idea how, but it would have to wait till morning. My biggest concern was that the formal investigation wouldn't look beyond the obvious. While still at the scene, some of the officers were already talking about murder-suicide. Tremayne all but labeled it in his report on KRVU.

The thought of the blowhard reporter brought back a scene from the dig. There'd been something between Adrienne and Tremayne . . . just the way they avoided each other. He barely interviewed her, and his usual banter was missing. He spent all his time with Bobby and the coeds. The coeds were no surprise, but was there a particular connection between Bobby and Tremayne, and even between him and Adrienne?

The scratching and whining at the back finally got through, and I rescued Shasta from the yard. As the dog rushed in, I bent down and grabbed her for a hug. Smiling slightly as the dog's pink tongue gave me a thorough face wash, I carried her to the bedroom and fell face-first into the pillows. After pulling up the spread, I barely moved a muscle. A fleeting thought zipped past . . . would I be plagued with bloody dreams?

Think happy thoughts. Think about buying shoes with Adrienne. Think about anything but tonight.

The mantra took up a rhythm, and I fell asleep, dreaming of Jimmy Choos and Louboutins.

The alarm sounded at 6:00 a.m. Groaning, I rolled to the edge of the bed. For the first few seconds, the horrors of the previous evening didn't exist. But I was still wearing work clothes, and they smelled of the morgue. It all came crashing back—the high from the great PR show of Gulf U students on their dig and the horror of the death of Adrienne and her student.

Even before getting the first hit of caffeine, I checked messages to make sure there were no calls from Max or the president. The twenty-plus calls were from media or curious friends, plus three others from Mother.

Coffee in hand, I clicked on the television, still tuned to KRVU. The newscaster was updating Houstonians on their latest shocking crime. He had all the sensationalism but nothing new in the facts department. I clicked it off. I swallowed the scalding coffee and skimmed my laptop programmed to get ten of the top local and national news feeds every morning. All of them had some mention of Gulf U and its latest tragedy.

After showering, I walked into the closet. Lining both walls were plastic shoe boxes. I sank to the ground. Hunching over my knees, I rocked back and forth. Unfurling myself, I picked up the nearest box, opening it to three-inch faux leopard sandals. I'd worn them once. Pulling out the right one, I pitched it over my shoulder. The left shoe followed, and then both candy-apple-red Jimmy Choos hit the bedpost. All I could think of was how I bonded with Adrienne over that first sale at Neiman's when we'd both grabbed the black stiletto Louboutins. Adrienne won and then offered to pay for coffee. I would never wear these again.

I knew I had to speak with Mother before facing the office. Whether it ended in screaming or crying or something in between, I didn't need it spreading over my office.

First I'd deal with my dog. Shasta had to be fed, watered, walked, and set for her day ruling the roost. The dog was content to sleep on the couch all day as the radio played in the background.

My neighbor was a godsend and walked her midafternoon. For once I envied my dog her peaceful routine.

With nothing else to keep me from calling Mother, I pushed the redial button on my call list. She must have been sitting with the phone in her hand, 'cause I swear it hadn't had time to ring even once when her face appeared on my phone.

"Well, thank God. You could have been killed for all I knew. I must have called you half a dozen times last night." Mother blasted me before I could even say hello.

"I'm fine, Mother. Just really tired and really sad. I didn't get home until after midnight and didn't want to disturb you. And frankly . . ." I pushed right through her attempt to admonish me. "Frankly, I couldn't talk with anyone. I had to go the morgue to formally identify Adrienne. Luckily, an officer drove me, because I'd never have gotten home on my own. I barely got Shasta back in the house before I collapsed."

Her screech could probably be heard a block away. "You had to do what? Identify her?"

I could hear her anger through the phone. I probably could hang up and still hear it—after all, she was only a half mile away.

Her tirade continued. "They had no right to make you do that. And what were you thinking to agree to something so horrible. Those people totally take advantage of your good nature. I'd have told them to go to hell. I'm sure Grace would have also."

Damn. I needed to call Grace before I went in as well. My daughter worked for the *Dallas Morning News.* I wouldn't be surprised if her editor hadn't already called her to track the inside story on the deaths.

"Mother, have you spoken to Grace? Does she know about Adrienne yet? I need to call her right now and make sure she's

OK. She liked Adrienne as much as I did." I was sure I was speaking ninety miles an hour.

"Hildegard, slow down. Grace is fine. She's a professional. She'll understand why you haven't called to fill her in. Why don't you come over tonight for dinner. We can drink a little wine and catch up on all of this. Bring Shasta. Minuit loves it when she visits."

In small doses, I thought.

With the phone set on speaker, I strolled across the room, collecting my purse, wool scarf and heavy jacket. Houston's usually balmy weather had given way to a cold front and a temperature in the low forties. My friends in Chicago always laughed when I complained about our short winter. It would be completely over by mid-March when the rodeo came to town.

"That would be great, Mother. See you tonight."

I'll send Grace a note. I didn't need an interview with her.

I texted her before I got distracted. *You've heard about Adrienne. Swamped now. Fill you in later. Love you.* Followed by a heart emoji.

I clicked send and headed to the office to face the ravenous horde.

I braced for the onslaught as I got to the office.

"Hey, Hildy, they've locked down Masterson Hall. You were there, right?" Joel March held out a cup of coffee as if this small kindness would buy him an inside scoop.

I ignored the offering and tried to move past.

Putting his hand on my arm, he continued. "I can't believe Dr. Harrington would do such a thing. She was such a nice woman.

Still waters run deep, I guess. They say it was a lovers' quarrel. Gotta feel sorry for the kid's family. You know?"

I glared until he pulled back his hand. He stepped back as I rushed into the administration building.

The prurient interest was the same I'd witnessed last night. Once again, I was in the know and for the moment the most popular person in the building. My heels clicked decisively as I moved down the marble hallway.

How dare Joel March intrude on the grief of others? And what about Adrienne's family and friends? Can't there be any sympathy for them?

In the few minutes it took for the ancient elevator to arrive to take me to the fifth floor and the president's office, I recaptured my composure and professional distance. I would need it to make it through the day.

The Akers Administration Building's polished green marble floors and matching striated granite walls were straight out of a 1930s art deco government building. But for once they didn't register for me at all. I walked deliberately across the stones, not only to keep from slipping on their highly polished surface but to minimize the *rat-a-tat* noise of high heels.

President Murphy's secretary, Mary Beth, looked up, her curious glance changing to sympathy. "Coffee?" she asked. I nodded. She sent the work-study student after one, and I took a chair, waiting for a summons into the inner sanctum.

My boss, Max Levine, was already on-site, his booming voice penetrating even through the closed door. He was a former radio newsman. He still had an unconscious habit of holding his hand to his ear when he was really concentrating. I was sure he'd been pulling at that ear a lot in the last hour.

Jeannell Bryant, the university's provost, was no doubt also present, along with President Murphy and the VP for Finance and Administration, Michael Graves. They'd probably been at it since before7:00 a.m. The clock showed 8:30, so hopefully the high-powered powwow was about to break up.

Chief West walked into the office just as the coffee arrived and Murphy's door opened. No time for speculation. Like it or not, my job was to help ensure the crisis ended as quickly as possible with the least possible long-term impact on the university. No real thought about finding justice or the truth. Just move the focus from the university. The only reason I was there. In times of catastrophe, the media handler became a valued commodity. It was true no matter who or where you were—corporations, government, the military, universities—we were ignored in the good times, screamed for in the bad.

"Hildy. Chief. Come in. Thanks for being so prompt." Murphy's hearty voice was appropriately subdued for the occasion.

"I know you've had a hard night, both of you. Hildy, I understand you had to formally identify Dr. Harrington at the morgue last night."

Max swung around and stared at me and then West.

I nodded, looking into the coffee cup to maintain a professional facade.

"Her family is very appreciative, and so are we, of course."

My head jerked up. "Her family?" My voice only slightly cracked. "I thought she had no family."

Murphy nodded. "Well, yes, no immediate family, not here anyway. But I've heard this morning from an aunt, I think her father's sister, in Virginia. Chief West's people tracked her down." He kept talking as he pawed through the loose papers on his desk. "Here it is. Angela Johnson. She hopes you can help with the arrangements as she won't be coming here."

All eyes turned in my direction—some sympathetic, all curious.

"Of course, I'll do anything I can for Adrienne." I rubbed my hands over the wrinkles in my black skirt. *I should have taken it to the cleaners last time I wore it.*

As I spoke, their eyes moved away, perhaps uncomfortable at any sympathetic reaction to Adrienne, a possible murderer, or even for the family of an alleged murderer. I would probably feel this distancing a lot over the next few weeks.

"Uh, that's fine, then." Murphy moved on.

"Chief, update us on what you've found, where we stand on this, then Hildy and Max, please outline what we need to do to keep this in check as much possible. Chief . . ."

"Sir." Chief West cleared his throat, looking over to Michael Graves, his boss, waiting for the nearly imperceptible nod to continue.

"Well, President Murphy, I gave Dr. Graves my report early this morning, after Hildy here finished with the media . . . and all." He glanced at me with a sympathetic crinkle at the corner of his eyes. "That report pretty much stands." He pulled out his tiny notebook, smaller even than a reporter's pad, and began reading.

"We have identified the other victim as Robert Earl Jake Jr., nineteen-year-old son of Texas state senator Robert Jake Sr. He was registered this semester as a junior honors student, lived in the athletics dorm, was a scholarship student in both athletics and social sciences, and was Dr. Harrington's student assistant for the past semester."

I jotted these same facts down as quickly as West read them off.

"Senator Jake came by early this morning and positively identified his son. We had to call a doctor, as he collapsed as he was leaving the viewing room at the morgue."

West barely nodded at me, acknowledging how hard it had been for me as well. I nodded back as he continued his report.

"We've got the murder weapon. It showed traces of blood from both Jake and Harrington. An antique dagger of some sort. Perhaps a relic from one of Harrington's archeological expeditions."

I looked up. Adrienne had an ornately carved knife in a case in her office that she'd brought back from a research dig in Japan. Not really an ancient relic, she'd said, sounding embarrassed at the touristy deal. She'd bought it in the street market from one of those young men who hawked wares in front of the hotels. Nonetheless, she believed it dated back to the eighteenth century. I would have to get Chief West to show me the weapon to make sure, but . . .

"—fingerprints only—"

"Uh, excuse me, Chief." I straightened up. "I think I missed part of what you were just saying. Could you repeat it please?"

"The dagger belonged to Dr. Harrington. Her hands were still gripped around the hilt of the knife. We found only her fingerprints on it. They were smudged, but we were able to get at least three clear prints. Enough to identify them positively.

"As I was saying, we've had time to interview Miss Brent, the cleaning crew member who found the bodies. She swears the office was locked. She used her passkey to get in. As soon as she turned on the light, she saw the bodies. She didn't touch anything before backing out and closing the door. She had the presence of mind to lock it again as she called campus police."

I continued taking notes as I built a picture from the chief's description.

That dagger was in her office, in a glass case. Anyone could have gotten hold of it. How hard was it to get into a faculty office? I couldn't let West wrap this up with Adrienne as the villain. There had to be another answer.

Five

ADRIENNE

Two Weeks after the Dig

IT WAS ALMOST DARK as Adrienne left her office in the Masterson Social Sciences Building. Dr. Minor had another week before she brought in her lawyer. She decided to call Mica to be ready, since she doubted the chairman would budge.

Tucking her bag under her arm, she picked up the pace. In a push to be a "pedestrian campus," all the parking lots were on the edges of the five-hundred-acre university. It was designed in concentric circles: core classroom buildings in the center, fanning out to professional schools, campus recreation facilities, dorms, public spaces, food services, and parking lots. Since her classes were primarily in the undergraduate quadrant, she had a few blocks to walk to her car.

She always smiled as she passed the fiberglass statue of Luis Jiménez's *Fiesta Dancers*. What a great symbol of the breadth of interests on this campus. She'd transferred here from the University of Virginia and loved how rich the city and its major university were.

No sooner had her mind touched on her former home than her worst nightmare was there, leaning on her car, smoking one of his ubiquitous Dunhill cigarettes. She was sure he thought he was channeling Hunter S. Thompson. He shouldn't have been able to find her.

"What are you doing here? How did you find me? My writ is still in effect. You are not supposed to be within five hundred yards of me." Her voice sounded shrill even to her.

Her ex-husband just blew smoke toward her. He smiled. "You are the one within five hundred yards of me. I'm just standing here."

His hand rubbed against her car, almost tenderly. "I wanted to see you . . . to see how you're doing in your new home, away from your family and friends."

Adrienne looked around, dismayed that the faculty parking lot was over half empty. There were security cameras, so they'd be able to tell Darrell was guilty if he tried anything, but that would be after she paid his price.

Tossing his cigarette butt on the ground, he pulled a gold Zippo lighter from his breast pocket, flipping open the top and putting it to the next cigarette without moving his eyes from her. His expression never changed.

"Look, Darrell. We settled all this in the divorce. I am no longer any concern of yours. These lots are monitored. All I have to do is scream, and Chief West and his men will be here in two minutes."

"A lot can happen in two minutes, my love." Darrell took another puff on his Dunhill.

Straightening up from his slouch, he stepped back a few paces and then turned toward the black vintage Camaro he'd babied for nearly twenty years. A gift from his father for being accepted to Princeton.

"Not to worry, babe. I'm just getting a feel for this place. Thinking of relocating."

Sweeping his eyes across the campus, taking in the music school and the science building, he smiled for the first time as he slid into the Camaro.

"I can see why you like it here. Yeah, Houston is a great place for an entrepreneur like me. I'll let you know where I settle. Don't want you to worry or anything."

Adrienne fell into her car, frantically pushing the lock button on the door as he drove across the lot. She grabbed the bottle of water and chugged half of it. Finally she pushed the on button for her Prius and slowly left the campus.

Adrienne fumbled for the key, digging through her shoulder bag until she felt it at the very bottom. Barely making it into her house, she locked the door and reset the alarm. Catrina stayed on the back of the couch, watching her human freak out.

She needed to breathe, and she needed a drink. Her fridge gave up a barely opened bottle of Provençal rosé, which she quickly poured into the wine glass on the counter . . . almost to the rim. Walking more slowly back to the couch, she carefully placed the glass on the sofa table and sank down into the corner. Catrina stared at her a moment before sidling over and rubbing her gray head against Adrienne's dark brown one. She rubbed the thick fur around the cat's neck. A half-inch of wine consumed and her calming pet at her side did much to settle her stomach.

"I should have changed my name. I was too easy to track. All he had to do was review anthropology faculty lists in colleges across the country. It took him nearly three years, but what good does that do me?"

Her fur rubbing got more strenuous, and Catrina started to pull away.

"Sorry, girl. Didn't mean to push you. But it makes me so mad and, yes, scared." *If I run again, I'll be totally starting over. Like witness protection. No teaching, no research, no Adrienne anymore.* Her brain refused to accept that.

"I'll be damned if I let him chase me away again."

Adrienne pulled the cat off the back of the couch and into her lap, drinking with one hand and petting with the other.

"Maybe Chief West can help. I need HPD to reissue the restraining order. I still have the X-rays of my broken arm. I need to find something to use against him. Yes. Maybe I can blackmail him into going away. Hildy and her team of student researchers might be able to help."

Standing up, she paced in front of the couch, the cat returned to the sofa back, watching her.

Three years ago she'd given up everything, including tenure, to be done with him. She'd escaped to Houston, even if she again had to fight for tenure at Gulf U. And it all started with that damn obscure manuscript.

She'd found it in the rare documents room at the Smithsonian Natural History Museum. It was a mirror of Darrell's dissertation on the original migration of the indigenous tribes into North America. The one he expanded into a book that got him tenure and the prestigious Gladstone Prize from the Royal Historical Society. She'd photographed it to show him, and he'd exploded.

Accusing her of jealousy that he had already been granted tenure, he grabbed her hand holding the telephone photograph, twisting her arm. The last thing she heard before fainting was a loud snap and the phone hitting the floor. She must have screamed, because when she came to, her neighbor Melanie was kneeling next to her. Darrell was long gone. A trip to the ER and a call to the Special Victims Unit of the Charlottesville PD resulted in charges being brought, a fast divorce, and the first restraining order.

Not enough evidence for a conviction, but once it was public, the university held a formal academic disciplinary hearing. In an unprecedented move, they revoked Darrell's tenure and fired him for cause. That started a year-long siege of harassment. She lost thirty pounds and looked anorexic. The final blow was when he showed up in her classroom and terrorized her students. She had an offer from Gulf State University that promised her tenure review within a year, and she jumped at it, leaving no forwarding address with anyone, even her rescuer, Melanie.

It had been a good move. Notwithstanding Gruesome Gus, she thought. She started working out regularly, regained her weight and her control. *I have friends I can count on. I'm not going to let him intimidate me again.*

Six

HILDY
Present

IT WAS A SLOW news day, or so I told myself as I checked out the twenty-two messages that were arranged on the desk in categories of descending importance.

National broadcast—1
Local broadcast, radio/TV—6
Local paper—3
Miscellaneous: mostly curious colleagues—7
Internet and exploitation media—5

Tearing up the bottom twelve, I read through names and locations for the other ten. It would take the rest of the morning to get back to all of these people, with nothing new to tell them.

I hit speed dial on the telephone console, and the ringing could be heard down the hall. Quickly pushing the sound level button, the noise was reduced to a one-room rattle. At times like these, I envied Carol's headset from the switchboard. As usual, I returned the calls with the speakerphone, hands free to continue rifling through mail and messages while the connections were being made.

I grabbed for the phone handset as soon as the polite voice on the other end answered, "Good morning. CBS Evening News. Can I help you?"

Will Mason was from Houston, as were some of his staff, so they kept pretty close tabs on what was happening in town. He'd attended some Gulf U classes while at the local CBS affiliate. Maybe he felt some kinship to the campus. At least that was the best I could come up with as to why his producer would be interested in this local tragedy.

"Yes, this is Hildy Brentwood at Gulf State University. I'm returning Phil Stewart's call."

"I'll connect you with the newsroom."

"News."

"Hello. I'm returning Mr. Stewart's call . . . Hildy Brentwood."

"Brentwood?" The voice on the phone was clearly not impressed. "OK, I'll see if I can find him . . . PHIL . . . call on two."

TV newsrooms were no different than newspaper bullpens—desks crammed up against each other, small file cabinets at each station, and papers piled floor to desk around every reporter's chair. It didn't take much imagination to picture the scene in New York. It was the same as Houston or LA, as was the indifferent response of the poor schmuck who was closest to the phone when it rang.

"Phil Stewart here. How can I help you?"

The broadcast quality voice pulled me back to reality.

"Hi Phil, this is Hildy. Hildy Brentwood. You know, at Gulf U in Houston. I'm returning your call."

Will Mason met with Gulf U students last year. Ethics and politics—one of those oxymoronic topics that journalists and journalism students love to chew on endlessly without changing a thing. Stewart had come with Mason to cover the talk for the Evening News. I was saddled with playing host to him and his crew for the day.

"Oh yeah. I called you, didn't I? Wait a minute. I wrote it down here somewhere. Oh yeah, that weird murder-suicide thing. I got flagged by a reporter at KRVU to check it out. Hey girl, you sure do interesting things out there in the Wild West! What's this all about? You know, this thing with the faculty bimbo and the Black kid . . . a basketball star, wasn't he?"

It had to be Jack Tremayne. No doubt pushing himself for network. Phil Stewart never covered local news, no matter how sexy the particulars were. OK, sure, maybe there was the pretty white female teacher and the young Black athlete angle, but this was no OJ thing. There were no celebrities, no national security interests, not even any grand pathos. Where was the national hook?

I pushed back to see just how interested he was. "Faculty *bimbo*? Drop the pseudo-cynicism, Phil. Here's what I can give you." My voice morphed into a neutral drone. I could have been talking about anyone, certainly not someone I'd shared so many personal laughs, tears.

"A little after 6:00 last night, the bodies of Dr. Adrienne Harrington and Robert Earl Jake Jr. were found on campus, both dead of apparent stab wounds. Time of death has been tentatively set at between 3:00 and 6:00 p.m. yesterday." I ticked off the data from the front of the police record.

"Harrington was a forty-two-year-old Caucasian, five foot ten, approximately one hundred thirty pounds. She taught anthropology at Gulf U for the last three years. She had a PhD from Cornell, and her masters and undergraduate degrees from Virginia Tech.

"Jake was nineteen. He was biracial, six foot ten, and about two hundred thirty-five pounds. He was an honors student majoring in political science. He also was starting quarterback on the Gulf State University Wolves football team. He was Dr. Harrington's student assistant for the past semester.

"The incident is being investigated by the Gulf U Police Department in cooperation with the Houston Police Department." My voice cracked slightly as I recited that piece of the clinical record.

As I was about to launch into the *Gulf U is a safe place and this has never happened here before* spiel, Stewart broke in.

"OK, OK, stop. I get the official picture. Heck, I already knew all that stuff. I got more than that off the tube last night." He paused for dramatic effect, lowering his voice into a conspiratorial whisper.

"Never would have looked if I hadn't been called by that reporter . . . Tremayne? Yeah. Said he has B-roll of the two of them in Costa Rica. So I thought I'd check it out. We go back a ways, Hildy. What's this all mean? What is really going on down there?"

In an equally secretive voice, I replied, "Well, actually Phil, it's all a communist conspiracy, a government cover-up, and the first attempt to control our minds by getting rid of any radical thinkers who might offer an intellectual argument against Armageddon when it comes, and we all know that's just around the corner. Dr. Harrington and Bobby Jake were the first who had to go because they represented everything that these pinko weirdos are against—our history and our sports!"

Stopping, I had to grin as I waited for the expected response. It was the first time I'd been able to joke about the horror. I had to keep this level of separation as I dealt with her friends and maybe-friends in the media.

"Very cute." He snorted, swallowing his laugh. "Really, it sounds too medieval. I mean, a ceremonial dagger, no less!"

Now how had he gotten that detail on the weapon? Which actually means where did Tremayne get that information? The only information reported so far was that a knife of some type was the weapon. Who had Jack been talking to?

"I don't know what you're talking about. Look, Phil, I'll try to keep you in the loop if you want, but I'm still not sure why. This isn't a national story. It's a local tragedy, sure. Hell, I'm sick to death about it. I knew them both, and they were good people. But there isn't anything here to interest you or Mason."

Getting no response, I pushed on. "So are you planning to run something about this tonight?"

"No, you're right. I don't see the national angle here."

Pumped my fist at his response.

"Let me know if something surfaces that might work for us."

I nodded and then answered smoothly that he was on my list. "I have your email on file and all your numbers."

We were at a clear stopping place in the discussion.

"Well, Hildy, old girl, you can't say your job is dull. Call me anytime, night or day, if something breaks."

"Now why did that conversation make me uneasy? Where the hell is Tremayne getting his information?" I didn't realize I spoke aloud until Amy, my assistant, poked her head in the office.

"Hildy, you OK?"

I nodded without speaking.

Amy stared and then continued. "OK, well, Mary Beth in President Murphy's office just called, and he wants you upstairs. Now."

At least I'd shut down the national interest. That should get me a point or two.

"She couldn't have done it!" I blurted out.

Five pairs of eyes turned. Chief West looked as if he would like to begin a fast interrogation to see if I actually might know something about the case.

"Pardon me, Hildy?" President Murphy asked softly. "Do you know something we should?"

Of course not. I stared back at him and shook my head, my defensiveness turning quickly to embarrassment.

"No, sir, not really. It's just that I know, er, knew Dr. Harrington, and I can't believe she'd do something like this." My already low voice dropped to almost a whisper.

"None of us can, and no one is saying she did, not without evidence. Right, Chief?" Murphy turned to West.

West nodded slowly. Everyone now looked equally embarrassed. I guessed that was because they already had leaped to a guilty or innocent conclusion, probably mostly guilty.

"All right then, we have much to do. We each have our own responsibilities to ensure Gulf State University does not suffer undue damage from these events."

President Murphy got back to the more comfortable, impersonal business at hand. All CEOs are basically cut from the same cloth—preserve the organization in times of crisis, and the human side will take care of itself. Murphy was a good CEO.

Jeannell Bryant was first up. She'd been provost and senior vice president for less than a year, coming to Gulf U from the University of Nebraska where she was dean of business. She hadn't had time to get to know all the twelve hundred faculty members and probably never met Adrienne Harrington at more than the get-acquainted reception in the fall.

The glass ceiling in universities was as difficult to shatter as at any Fortune 500 company, maybe tougher. Dr. Bryant was among the first harbingers of the twenty-first century at an institution where non-white, non-male academic and administrative managers were counted in the low double digits.

It wasn't surprising that Gulf U's first female senior appointment would come from a business school. A national expert in organizational behavior, Dr. Bryant looked like she belonged in a boardroom. She dressed more conservatively than the other VPs or even the president, all of whom had succumbed recently to a gaudy tie fad. Bryant's gray pin-striped suit and starched white blouse was captured at the throat with a gold circle pin. Her dark brown hair was cut short, away from her face, and her serious brown eyes were framed by tortoise-rim glasses.

Her formal attire was matched by her manner, and only President Murphy seemed comfortable calling her by her first name. I certainly never would. Nonetheless, I did know that Dr. Bryant was one of the most wickedly funny women around. Her sense of humor was biting, sarcastic, tinged with the slings and arrows she no doubt dodged on her way to her present position. I learned this well-guarded secret during our first interview, while she was still in Nebraska. We spent some great time crafting her press release and inventing answers to the predictable questions like "What does it feel like to be the first female top academic administrator at the state's major public urban university?"

The first three of her answers were unprintable, and the next three ranged from thanking the reigning male establishment for giving her this unprecedented opportunity to the finally acceptable perspective that she hadn't ever considered this a groundbreaking appointment, only one she was eminently qualified to assume.

So as I looked over to her, there was a certain sympathetic cast to her eyes—or did I just want to see it there? Her voice certainly contained nothing of it, as Dr. Bryant outlined the actions that she and Dean Garner had taken that morning to protect her college, her faculty, her students.

"We canceled those classes that Dr. Harrington was scheduled to teach, and we'll have a substitute in by the end of next week to take over." She looked down at her iPad, checking off her list. "We may have to go outside the department until we can run a search for her replacement."

Everyone nodded wisely. I paused in my frantic note-taking to wonder if perhaps I'd misjudged the warmth and sympathy I'd felt earlier. Bryant was operating in corporate hyperdrive.

"We've also arranged for Dr. O'Neal to provide counseling services to any of Dr. Harrington's students, particularly those who went with her on the recent dig . . . and of course to the members of the football team or anyone else on campus who needs help dealing with this . . . incident," Bryant continued in a monotone litany of jobs completed.

I was glad to hear the students were already being looked after and made a mental note to call Dr. O'Neal as soon as the meeting was finished. At least there was one task to mark off the list. Now the list was only two pages long.

"Thanks, Jeannell. That relieves one of my worries." Dr. Murphy quickly moved to less-controlled areas. "So, Max, Hildy, what else should we think about? What do we have to look forward to with our friends from the media?"

Max and I had an unwritten agreement—he left all the media relations and strategy to me, and I supported him on his push for increased communication within the campus. Gulf U certainly needed both now.

He straightened in his chair. He always had a crumpled, well-worn newsman's look about him. After fifteen years in radio, he moved to corporate communications in the oil industry before settling down ten years ago in the quiet halls of academe. He no doubt believed he'd be getting a semiretirement marked by home-comings and graduations.

In reality the halls were neither quiet nor all that high-minded. The university was a small town with lots of small businesses (the colleges and departments), individual entrepreneurs (the faculty), and the occasional disgruntled customers and citizens (the students and alumni). It had all the civic responsibilities for safety, health, and economic viability, and it ran its own telephone and electrical generating systems.

In my opinion, Gulf U and Max had the perfect marriage. His idea of a good time was the lifeblood of a university—the committee meeting. It may be tough to get things done quickly, but it sure made a difference in how many people played a role in the decision. In higher education they called it shared governance. In business it was labeled indecisiveness.

Max was right though. The students, faculty, and staff were at least as important an audience as the legislature or donors or downtown business leaders.

So it was no surprise his response was couched in how to get information to the campus community and how to make everyone feel safe.

"Well, Paul, last night, right after we got word from the chief, we sent out the crime announcement to all offices through voice and email to get to all faculty and administrative staff. We initiated the emergency notification system to the students through their voice and emails and emergency links. At that point we didn't know if there was still a danger to the campus. The police shut down the campus, and everyone was told to stay in their offices and dorms. The fact that this happened in daylight has got a lot of folks spooked.

"Today you need to issue a quick statement to the campus community about increased security and that all immediate danger has passed. I don't need to tell you we need to get this solved as quickly as possible." Max spoke faster when he was particularly concerned.

He didn't look over to Chief West, but everyone else did.

President Murphy nodded automatically, looking at the chief with the unasked question.

West sounded only a little defensive as he stared right back. "You know, sir, we can't tell at this point how long the investigation will take. We've got four of our best people on it and think we can resolve it in an expeditious manner." He sounded more bureaucratic than usual.

Max brought up the subject many of them were thinking. "Chief, none of your guys has much experience with this kind of thing. Wouldn't we be better off turning this over to Houston PD? From a PR perspective, I think we would."

I had to agree. Jurisdiction was precious in the law enforcement business.

Before West could answer, his boss, Michael Graves, stepped in. "Mr. President, Max." He was smiling, no doubt humoring the PR flacks. "The chief has had more than twenty years in homicide in LA, and his men are fully trained. They are graduates of the FBI training school, which is more than most of HPD."

I had to respond. "Of course, absolutely. It's just that we have some involvement here. We may even have some liability, if it proves that Adrienne really did commit . . . this . . . act." I couldn't bring myself to say murder. "And HPD was on the scene last night. Aren't they working with you on the investigation, Chief? I thought that's what you said yesterday."

Before West or Graves could jump in with a sharp answer, President Murphy recaptured the conversation.

"All right, everyone. This isn't getting us anywhere. Hildy, why don't you go over the press stuff. Do we need to do anything this morning? Do I need to issue any other statement?"

I focused on the strong face of the president. He was molded after the quintessential academic administrator. Medium tall and still in pretty good shape, his dark hair now was a shade of steel gray and as full as if he were still in his forties. He wore it in a conservative cut, short on the sides but longish on the top. Black frames either hid or accentuated his blue eyes, depending on his mood. Today, his blue eyes looked more the color of his hair.

"We issued a statement from your office last night. There's a copy on your desk, but it was the standard crisis communication stuff. I have a mountain of messages on my desk, which I'll answer when we're through. I have already spoken with CBS. The Nightly News producer called. I promised to add him to our media distribution for this. I think Tremayne at KRVU flagged him about it, trying to get network airtime."

The finance VP jumped in. "It might be the rumor that Robert Jake plans to run for governor."

Graves held up his phone where he'd googled Jake to find a website touting a possible gubernatorial run for the state senator.

That might explain it, I thought as I continued.

"We'll hear from everyone we didn't hear from last night, as well as the faithful who got here yesterday. They'll be swarming all over the place, talking to students, faculty, anyone who knew either of them. Chief . . ." I looked over at the large, silent man. "I may need some of your people to be physically present in the Social Sciences building, near the classrooms and offices, just to make sure no one violates any students' rights or walks into any classes uninvited."

West nodded and made a quick note in his small book.

"The press will want an update, with confirmation on the identifications and details on the investigation," I continued. "We'll set up a briefing room near my office to keep them out of the academic buildings as much as possible. As a public facility, we can't ban them from the campus, but we can definitely keep them out of the classrooms and labs and definitely the dorms."

I finished my analysis without looking at the chief. "The media are going to keep focusing on Gulf U and possible relationships as long as the investigation is going on, and frankly, Dr. Murphy, as long as we are running that investigation, we are going to have them swarming all over the place."

"Yes, I can imagine," he responded, a frown creasing his forehead.

"Well, we all have a great deal to do. Let's get on with it. Max, get the internal messages out as quickly as possible. I sure don't want people scared to come to work. Speaking of which, Michael, would you make sure the poor custodian who discovered . . . the bodies . . . is OK? See that she gets counseling if she needs it." They both nodded.

"Can we give her some time off? You know, administrative or sick leave?" I asked.

When they looked at me curiously, I finished the thought. "I'd sure hate to see her turn up on *America Undercover* or one of those programs. If she's still on campus, they're likely to try to track her down."

The group nodded.

"Of course, we can't stop her from talking if she chooses to, but maybe if she's off visiting a sister or cousin out of town, it will have died down before that would happen."

"Yes, look into that, too, Michael, will you?" Murphy asked.

Again, a brief nod from the vice president. He seemed to be waiting to ensure that his police force was still controlling the investigation.

"Chief West," Murphy continued. "You and your men did an admirable job last night. You may continue with your work. But keep HPD and the DA's office fully informed, and if you can't bring it to a satisfactory conclusion by next week, I really think we need to turn the lead over to the city." He looked at West and then Graves, who nodded.

Murphy then turned and began scrutinizing the papers on his desk. No one needed to be told we were dismissed.

"Amy, everyone has their assignment. I don't want to be disturbed for the next hour, unless it's Max or the president . . . or Chief West."

Without waiting for an answer, I closed my door, one of the few times in my twenty-plus years at Gulf U. A shut door sent a closed-off message I didn't like. But that policy meant I rarely had time to think without interruption. And I needed time to think . . . time to figure a strategy to find an answer to the deaths that did not include Adrienne as the murderer, while at the same time getting murder at Gulf U off the front pages of the tabloids and blogs.

I settled into the leather ergonomic chair that I'd dragged from office to office. It didn't give me a backache. I had my favorite Mickey Mouse note pad, with Mickey subtly embossed on the cover. Perfect for academic meetings, which often devolved into minutia and fantasy.

Pushing aside the unread magazines and newspapers, I was left with a laptop docked into a large-screen display. I knew I was messing with my space to avoid thinking.

Such a coward. It would be so easy to just go along. To give the media the bare facts and let them assume what they will. Truthfully, that would get us off the front page the fastest.

"But it would be a lie."

I flicked a pen against the still blank page, my desktop now cleared of all extraneous distractions. My eyes sought out the painting of the old woman weaving a basket with the golden heat of the desert shimmering around her like a halo. I'd bought it at the Indian Market two summers ago when Adrienne and I had vacationed in Santa Fe. It wasn't the only reminder. The abstract statue of a woman's torso anchored the corner near the window . . . another art piece we'd found. That had been the piece that also introduced me to my friend Abby, who owned the Heights gallery on Nineteenth.

Staring out the window, I could see six crows roosting in the large oak tree that filled the panes. I think they called that a *murder of crows*. I could have been back in the jungles of Costa Rica if I squinted my eyes tight and let my imagination loose. "Stop. You have to concentrate. What can you do, and without Max or Chief West squashing it?"

And here I was, talking to myself, without Shasta for a cover. Glad I'd shut the door so Amy wouldn't think I'd gone over the edge, yelling at myself. Lists. I needed to make a list of tasks to complete.

- ✓ Check on getting a copy of police and coroner's reports
- ✓ Interview the student blog team about Bobby Jake and what he was into
- ✓ Look through Adrienne's house to see if she left any clues on what she was doing with Bobby Jake in her office

At the thought of Adrienne's cottage, I threw down the pen and picked up my phone.

"Could I speak with the chief? This is Hildy Brentwood."

"Hildy, everything OK?"

"Yes, Chief. Hanging in there. Just trying to work through it all. It dawned on me that I don't know what happened with Adrienne's cat. Has someone rescued her?"

West's voice leveled off. "I believe her neighbor is feeding her for the moment. Why?"

I'd found my way into Adrienne's house. "Well, I can keep her with me until her aunt decides what to do. She, I mean the cat, and Shasta, my dog, get along great, so she'd not feel so displaced. I can swing by and pick up her things this afternoon if you can clear me to get in her house. I already have a key."

"You don't need me to get in the house. It's been cleared by the crime scene guys. Wish I'd known you had a key. I had to pick the lock."

Holding my phone with my shoulder, I pulled out my bag and slid the Mickey Mouse notepad into the side flap. "Great. Thanks, Chief. I know Catrina will feel a lot better."

"Catrina?"

Juggling the phone as I walked to the door, I almost smiled. "Yes, Catrina . . . the cat. Thanks again." Hitting the red end button, I pushed the phone into the bag, glad to have something tangible to do beyond fielding media calls.

Seven

I CRACKED OPEN ONE eye and immediately slammed it closed. Even the smallest hint of light exploded and threatened to short out everything. I was lying on a thin mattress or heavy blankets. Afraid to move a muscle. Very slowly, I flexed my feet. No broken ankles. Legs were probably OK. Trying the same movement with my wrists, I inched my right arm across my torso, touching my elbow, resulting in a sharp pain.

Don't try that again.

My left side felt bruised, and my left arm was useless. Just touching it caused a lightning bolt of pain. Very slowly I squinted, registering light from small windows high in the wall. As the room quit spinning, I looked up at a track with a chain running toward the front windows.

Damn.

I wanted to shake my head and clear my brain—bad idea. Without turning my head, I tried to see the side walls. A saw and hammers, a bench with a vice, two shovels leaning against the wall. The smell of kerosene, motor oil, and mud filled my nose and stomach.

Adrienne's house. I came to pick up the cat and look around. I used the key she'd given me. What a mess. Did the cops leave it this way?

I remembered walking inside. A sharp pain to the back of my head was all I recalled. *At least I'm not tied up.* A quick glance down showed my clothes were intact. So rape was probably not the motive.

Please don't let me throw up, at least not until I can find a bucket.

Carefully rolling to my right side, I looked around the small garage. The thin mattress was an old dog bed, covered in gray and black fur. I was up against the wall on the raised ledge that also housed a washer and dryer. Sitting still for five minutes ensured my stomach stayed in one place and my head quit spinning. Now to maneuver into an upright position with only one arm and less-than-perfect knees.

Another ten minutes passed as I scooched over to the washer, pressed my back against the solid white machine, and pushed oh so slowly to an upright position. Then another few minutes grabbing on to the washer to ensure my balance. Falling back down was not an option.

Most garages in the neighborhood had only a main door. Leaning against the dryer, I moved over to the garage door button. I pushed it. Then pushed it again. Whoever put me here must have taken the opener and locked the mechanism. But Adrienne's garage had a side door on the left past the workbench. It made it easier to get to the laundry from the main house. Holding on to the dryer and then the workbench, I reached the door tucked away on the side. If my left arm were working better, I would have crossed my fingers as I slipped my right thumb and middle finger into the small pocket in my jeans.

YES. They (whoever they were) didn't find the key.

The key fit in the deadbolt, and the door was well-oiled. Moving slowly and as silently as possible, I moved across the deck to the back door. Looking through the window, I realized a hurricane had been through the house, or someone looking for something in a great hurry. It was painful, but I somehow felt triumphant. For the first time I had proof that there was more to the story than murder-suicide.

Trying not to touch anything despite needing to sit or fall down, I headed for my purse on the hall table. Remarkably, it was still there. Dropping it there was the last thing I remembered—before finding myself in the garage.

Walking slowly along the edges of the room, I leaned against the door and pulled out my phone. Chief West's number was the top on the redial list, so I didn't need to search for it.

"Chief West, please . . . this is Hildy."

"Hildy? Can't you get in the house?" His voice sounded like he was in the middle of something. Not too surprising.

"Chief? I need you to come out here. To Adrienne's. Someone has trashed the place."

My voice sounded strained, even to me.

"Are you OK? What's happened?"

I heard him scooting back from his desk.

"Yeah, guess so. Still kind of woozy, and I have a knot on the back of my head. But mostly OK."

Sliding down the door to the floor, I hugged my knees and rocked a little.

"We're on our way, along with the EMTs. Stay on the line, and we'll be with you in less than five minutes."

He kept talking until I heard sirens in the near distance. I felt safe knowing he was coming.

"You're sure you're all right?" Chief West stared as if he could see my bones and muscles to assess any injury.

"Fine. I'm just fine." That was all I'd been saying for the thirty minutes since the police had roared into the neighborhood and onto Adrienne's driveway. They were still going through the damaged rooms, and the garage had been blocked off as a crime scene since that's where I'd been locked up by whoever had trashed the house.

"What the hell were you doing here, anyway?" West's voice dropped almost to a growl.

"Catrina. I was here to get the cat, remember? I called and got your OK."

He nodded and touched the edge of the squad car door where I sat, having tolerated the EMTs exam and refused transportation to the ER.

"I barely got the door open, and it was lights out. Don't know how I ended up on a dog blanket in the grungy garage. Hell, I didn't even know Adrienne ever had a dog. And I still haven't gotten hold of Catrina."

Like the diva she was, the cat made her entrance right on cue, coming out from the patio door to the car. She launched herself into my lap, curled around once, and settled down.

"Well, that solves that problem." My fingers twisted through the steel-gray fur, a surprisingly comforting act.

"There is one bright note from all this." Still smoothing the fur on the cat's back, I looked up at Chief West.

"Adrienne didn't knock me on the head. Someone was searching for something, probably something she didn't have on her or in her office."

I moved too fast, closing my eyes to the sharp pain. The vertigo was thankfully gone, but the headache would stay for a while.

"Whatever they wanted, it got her killed and Bobby with her. Adrienne was murdered, Chief. She's not the killer."

West shook his head, staring into my eyes to determine whether the hospital was called for.

"That's pure speculation, Hildy. We know nothing of the kind. As far as I can tell, this is a burglary gone wrong. You were in the wrong place at the wrong time. Thieves pay attention to deaths in the media and target those empty houses. This was a crime of opportunity. They took the flat-screen, her jewelry. Would have gotten her laptop and phone except we already had those."

I slowly moved my head left to right.

"No. This was the murderer. He was looking for something and stole those things to throw you off."

West squatted next to me, touching my hand. "I'll ask HPD to increase drive-bys of the neighborhood for a few nights, OK? In the meantime, you're going to the ER. I don't want to hear another word. You are in pain and were totally out of it for ten minutes or more.

"Officer Taylor, round up the cat paraphernalia and put it in my trunk, please. See if there is a carrier anywhere so we can secure her while Hildy gets checked out."

He turned his iron gaze back to me. "Now hear this clearly, Hildy. Stop whatever you are doing. Let us do our job . . . and you do yours. You are not to put yourself in danger again." At that he waved over his officer standing to the side, his arms full of cat stuff.

A minute later I was huddled in the corner of a police car heading somewhere I didn't want to go.

Eight

I FINALLY MADE IT home with a bandage covering a shaved part of my skull and a small gray cat huddled in the back of a carrier. I'd turned down the pills the ER doc was pushing. I didn't want anything that would make me fuzzy, so I settled for the new mix of Advil and acetaminophen I had at home. Thankfully, the docs cleared my arm as a sprain, which already felt better.

I couldn't believe it was still daylight. I had about thirty minutes before my summons to Mother's grand Victorian home. Shasta heard my car and started barking before I reached the porch. "OK, OK. Calm down. Let me get in, and I'll give you a good rub."

I wrestled my way inside, keeping my knee against the door to prevent the eager dog from shooting outside. I automatically dropped my purse on the side table and my coat on the chair by the door. Shasta discovered her friend Catrina in the carrier just inside the doorway. She immediately dropped into her downward dog yoga pose, wiggling her butt with her nose pressed against the mesh.

"Hey. I thought I was the highlight of your day." I grinned at the beasts and their joy with each other. My smile softened as I thought of my friend and how much better this would be if she were here with us. "Catrina, I swear I'll get answers for your cat mom." I sent my best vibes to the animals and into the cosmos, praying that my declaration would prove true.

Time to clean up before presenting myself at Mother's. Maybe Catrina would divert some of the angst about my safety as we determined where the cat should go. Wishful thinking. Mother had always been hyper-protective, in her own professional way. But in the years following my father's hit-and-run death, she watched both me and now Grace like the proverbial hawk.

There was a fine line of appropriate wardrobe when visiting Mother. This should be a jeans and shirt visit, but I opted for wool slacks and a cashmere twinset she'd given me for Christmas. How did I even know what a *twinset* was? But the soft gray wool felt great, so I couldn't complain. At least my choice of clothes wouldn't come up over dinner.

I left Catrina in the carrier while I changed, with Shasta trying to lick her through the mesh. Fifteen minutes later, I was properly attired, coated, and scarfed with a cat carrier in one hand and a leashed Shasta in the other. Too many things to maneuver on a half-mile walk, so I loaded us up in my Subaru, arriving in Mother's drive before the heater had fully engaged.

Victoria Ridley Brentwood's home was more a grand Southern plantation than the quirky Victorians seen throughout the rest of the Heights, or Galveston, or New Orleans, or San Francisco, for that matter. Her landscape mirrored her Southern royalty vision—magnolia trees, white oak leaf hydrangeas, lilies, and white azaleas. Alyssum trailed down the planter boxes, and the fragrance of gardenias and star jasmine floated across the lawn spring through summer.

It gave the illusion of cool tranquility, on the hottest August day or the grayest day in January. As much as I resented my Junior League mother, I loved the peace I always found in her garden. In a small way, I brought that same feeling to my backyard with my touch of wildly colorful fountains, whirligigs, and glass bells. I liked my serenity with a bit of whimsy and chaos.

Minuit met us at the door, wiggling so hard she could barely stand up. Mother had rescued the black greyhound from Gulf Greyhound Racetrack in 2020 when it closed down. They were inseparable. Mother even took her to the foundation when she had a board meeting, one of the perks of being chair of the board of Houston Charities Foundation—once they were meeting in person again.

Happily Catrina had already met Minuit at a few events at my house, so I had no worries about letting her loose. As fastidious as Mother was, she was always tolerant of animal hair.

"Mother, we're here." I could hear her in the kitchen and headed that way. She walked out holding two glasses of white burgundy.

Mother barely acknowledged me, speaking with a soft cooing. "I heard a cat crying so I had to come investigate. She's a beauty, Adrienne's Russian Blue, right?"

The cat was currently batting at Shasta's nose through the mesh.

"I rescued her after everything. She gets along with Shasta, but I'm not sure I can keep her."

Mother gave me her *shame on you* look. "You can't just give her away. She's been traumatized. She needs proper care and attention. You need to find her a good home."

Nodding, I freed the cat from the carrier. "I plan to, Mother. I just need to speak with Adrienne's aunt to make sure she doesn't want her. She lives in Virginia, so I'm guessing she'll want me to find a home for her. But I have to check." Catrina was weaving her way between Mother's ankles, her purr on full throttle. Minuit and Shasta were watching her closely. She'd already showed them her claws to establish proper alpha status.

Dinner was set up in Mother's sunroom—chicken salad and her famous grilled fruit kebobs. An unspoken agreement held that we'd not discuss the grisly details while eating.

Two hours later, with Mother fully briefed, my head injury thoroughly examined, and with a forceful warning about staying out of trouble, I dragged my motley crew back to the bungalow. If I was lucky, they'd let me sleep until seven, but I wasn't going to hold my breath.

My headache felt like a sore tooth. Nonetheless, I was back at work. Mica persuaded me to honor our monthly standing lunch. I had to hurry to keep up with her as she strode toward Martha Blue's Café. Being six inches shorter was a distinct disadvantage when Mica was in power mode. We'd driven across town to get away from the depressing cloud that hung over Gulf U since the deaths. The café had amazing quiche and was just down from Abby's gallery.

"I can't believe you dragged me to your neighborhood for lunch." Mica stopped in front of the restaurant's blue door. "I have to be back at the law school by two, and since when do you take ninety-minute lunches?"

I patted her arm, knowing that Mica liked to blow with no real animosity.

"You'll love this place. It's quiet so we can talk, and the food is wonderful. Abby discovered it. She's going to introduce us to the chef/owner."

Mica turned with a scowl pulling her shapely eyebrows into a *V*. She was a striking woman with dark brown hair highlighted with gold. Her nearly six-foot height got an added three inches from her suede boots. She easily ignored the stares, as she had the looks of a runway model and the brains of a fierce litigator.

"I wish you'd warned me you were including that hippie for lunch. I'd have stayed back to work on Blair Prescott's contract with CMA records."

I scowled back. "Be nice. Abby is fun, and she found this place. Look, she already has a table for us so no waiting in line. You can get back to your contract faster."

Waving, I pushed to the front of the line and flagged the hostess. She marched us through to the back of the room where Abby was drinking a Virgin Mary. Her blonde hair looked like she'd dried it with a leaf blower. Her flowered gauze blouse was covered with a handwoven vest.

"Just in time. I pulled my chef connection to get seated in advance. You'll love this place. The chef is a hunk. Hildy, you need to pay particular attention."

Sliding into the banquette, I shook my head. "Abby, stop trying to fix me up with every hetero man you meet. You should be looking for someone to share your life, not mine."

Turning to Mica, Abby carefully chose which button to push. "So, Mica, what's the news with the Kardashians? I haven't seen

People magazine this week, so what's happening in the glitter world? What scandals are you covering up for your clients?"

Abby grinned, knowing she'd lit Mica's fireworks.

"How many times must I explain? I do not hang out with celebrities. I do not cover up scandals. And I wouldn't know a Kardashian from a Neanderthal. I teach law and the intricacies of communication and entertainment contracts. My private clients are local performers needing legal advice on setting up their businesses." Mica settled down onto the sueded booth seat. "Enough bullshit. I want to see this miraculous quiche. It better not be full of buckwheat or tofu or matcha tea or any of that other vegan food you love."

Abby just grinned. "OK. Hildy, how are you are doing? How's your noggin? It's been days since Adrienne died, and I still see the tragedy every night on KRVU. Can't they find some scandal or something else to follow?"

I hunched up my shoulders in a futile attempt to get some of the stress worked out. "Hell, they have the bit in their teeth and don't seem to want to let go. I think Tremayne hopes this will take him to the network. We're about to turn the investigation over to HPD, which may take some of the heat off."

Abby looked confused. "That's a good thing, right? So why do you look so sad."

My hands kept pleating the cloth napkin. It would have been shredded if it had been paper. I almost whispered my response.

"I think they'll try to wrap this up quickly, and that means they'll close the case with Adrienne identified as the killer who then turned the knife on herself. And that is not what happened. I just don't have anything to prove it. You would have thought my being attacked at her house yesterday would have at least suggested someone else might be involved."

Abby's eyebrows were lost in her bangs. I hadn't shared my adventure with her yet. I raised my hand to indicate I'd fill her in later.

Mica shook her head. "Bet they blamed it on random robbers taking advantage of an empty house." I nodded and then moaned. *Note to self—move head slowly when agreeing with someone until further notice.*

The waitress interrupted, and we ordered the quiche and salad with Arnold Palmers.

Once she'd left, Mica reached over and touched my arm. "You know, Adrienne visited me last fall. I guess I can share this without violating privilege. She said she needed help in finding someone . . . a person adopted through a private arrangement twenty years ago. It didn't take much to figure out she was the mother who gave up her child."

I started to stand and was pulled back down by Abby. My voice hit a higher-than-normal register. "And you're just telling me this now? Mica, this could be really important. Did you tell Chief West?"

Shaking her head, she responded, "It never occurred to me, and no one asked. But I remembered the other day that we talked about ways to find an adopted kid. I suggested she register her DNA on Ancestors.com in case the now adult child was also trying to find his mother. It was clear she was talking about herself. She didn't have any documentation from the lawyer and couldn't remember his name. All she knew was the child was a boy. Her parents handled all the arrangements. They are both dead, and she couldn't locate any documents among their papers. I think she was considering hiring a private detective."

Mica took a long drink of her lemonade and iced tea. The quiche arrived at that moment, so we went silent.

I broke the silence with small talk while worrying about what her revelation might mean. "Abby, you're right, this is great quiche."

"Uh. Is that all you have to say?" Mica lightly poked me, and I gave in.

"I'm in shock. You guys hardly knew each other. So why tell you her deep, dark secret?"

"Hello. Lawyer here. I was helping her fight Gruesome Gus in her tenure battle. So get over it. Are you really going to fixate on the fact that I know something you don't about your friend? She came to me because I'm the only lawyer she knew and she had legal questions."

I raised my hand in apology. "You're right. Sorry, it just hit me hard. So Adrienne had a child. A son, right? That's what you said."

Mica nodded as I pushed on.

"That can't be a coincidence. It has to mean something. Could that be what she was so worried about last week? I thought it was her fight with Gus Minor. I even thought she might have had a bad run-in with Jack Tremayne. I know they met before our Costa Rica trip 'cause she kept as far away from him as possible on the dig. I don't know. This keeps getting murkier and murkier. I still haven't reached Adrienne's aunt in Virginia. I've left messages. Maybe she can clear some of this up."

I fumbled in my purse for a credit card. "This one's on me, ladies. You've just given me a clue that might unravel this whole thing."

We finished our drinks. No one felt like dessert after thinking about Adrienne, so we stood and headed out the door.

Abby stopped us on the walk. "Don't forget you promised to make my opening next Monday. We'll have wine and nibbles, you know, the usual. You'll love the two artists I'm showing—a photographer and a sculptor. Both brilliant. Mica, you should come too."

I was surprised when Mica slowly nodded her head. Another shock. Did Mica like art?

Never mind. I had enough to think about as I drove back to campus. Now I really needed to talk with Adrienne's aunt.

Nine

WITH MICA'S NEWS, I was more determined than ever to speak with Adrienne's aunt. I almost had her number memorized. I tapped it into my phone once more. Persistence pays off. "Mrs. Johnson? This is Hildegard Brentwood from Gulf State University. I've been trying to reach you."

"Oh my. Yes. President . . . Murphy, is it? He told me you would call. I apologize. I've been so upset I haven't returned any calls . . . too many reporters and gossips. Ms. Brentwood, you are . . . were a friend of Adrienne's?"

I pushed back in my chair, straightening my spine. "Please, call me Hildy. Adrienne was a good friend. I'll be happy to help you in any way I can."

"I'm Angela. Call me Angela. You'd think I'd be better at this after burying my parents and my brother, Adrienne's father, and his wife. But I'm just as frazzled as when John died. Both John and Adrienne's mother were killed in a car accident. Adrienne was still at home after her trauma at University of Virginia."

Looking down at the folder with Adrienne's background information, I flipped to the copy of her curriculum vitae, the academic version of a resume. Virginia Tech was listed as her undergraduate university. "Angela, I want to be sure and get all of Adrienne's information correct. I thought she got her BS degree from Virginia Tech."

"Yes, of course. She started at Virginia and then dropped out at the start of her junior year. She eventually finished up at Virginia Tech."

I should have FaceTimed the call so I could see Angela's face. It might have helped me figure out what she meant.

"Eventually? Did she stop for a bit before returning?"

Angela hesitated a second and then rushed ahead. "Just a bit. But she bounced right back after everything. She enrolled at Virginia Tech and finished up in record time, graduating with honors. They awarded her a research assistantship and full scholarship for her master's. She then got a fellowship at Cornell where she got her doctorate. Adrienne was an outstanding scholar. Actually I was a bit surprised when she accepted the assistant professorship at Virginia, but I guess it had always been her Shangri-la."

Looking up, I caught sight of the artwork I'd bought on a trip to Santa Fe with Adrienne. My throat got tight for a second before continuing.

"You're right, she was a great scholar and a wonderful teacher. Angela, a friend of mine mentioned that Adrienne had asked her about tracking adopted children. Did she have a baby?"

Angela's voice broke a bit. "Well, I know you were her good friend. I don't think she spoke much about it, although there was a police investigation, so there may be a record somewhere."

Using a favorite reporter trick, I kept silent, hoping Angela would feel the need to fill the empty space.

"I guess it no longer matters. Adrienne must have needed to get it all out if she was confiding in your friends. You see, she was raped at a fraternity party the start of her junior year. They drugged her or something, and she was attacked by a number of them."

"Oh my God!" I gripped the phone, biting my tongue to keep from yelling as Angela continued.

"They dropped her at her dorm, in pretty bad shape, remembering very little. Her roommate got her to the infirmary where they determined she'd been raped. Police were notified, but since she had no real memory of anything after she got to the party, there was little that could be done. Twenty years ago universities tended to cover this stuff up. She came home. A month later she realized she was pregnant."

Angela was almost whispering. I couldn't tell whether someone else was with her, but she clearly didn't want this secret spread. "Her parents insisted she give up the baby and arranged for a private adoption. Shortly after, her parents were killed in a car accident. She had a lot to deal with and stayed with me a few months. We were all devastated but wanted to do anything we could to support her. She transferred to Virginia Tech the next semester. We never spoke about it. At the time it seemed like the best. I'm not sure Adrienne always agreed with that. I think she thought often about her lost son. I'm not surprised she was looking for him."

Angela's voice got stronger as she pushed ahead.

"But that has nothing to do with today. Again, I am so grateful that you will help with the arrangements. I'll want to bring her back to Virginia to be buried with her parents in the family plot, but if you think we should do something for her friends in

Houston, let me know. I don't know when the police will release her to us, so anything we do will need to be virtual."

I had to get a grip. I shook all over trying to pull back into my professional persona. "Of course, whatever you want. There are some friends I was thinking of pulling together to raise a glass in her memory. We'll do it at my place or maybe a favorite restaurant. I'll be glad to FaceTime you in if you want. As to the official arrangements, I can notify you as soon as the police can release her to you. You have my number now, so please call me if you need anything or have any questions."

Angela responded to my sudden formality with a similar tone. "Thank you very much. I appreciate your help. I would like to know how they're doing with the investigation. The reporters have suggested that Adrienne did this. I can't believe she would do anything violent. If she were going to hurt someone, it would have been her ex. He was the one threatening her, and all she would do is get a restraining order. She wouldn't even carry a gun for protection."

I was nodding through the conversation until the part about Adrienne's ex. "Angela, I knew Adrienne had been married before, but why would her ex want to hurt her?"

"Bless her heart, if that girl didn't have bad luck, she'd wouldn't have had any luck at all. She met her husband, Darrell, in grad school. They married quickly. She believed their common research passion would translate into something more personal.

"Five, or maybe six years later, he was working on a postdoc, and she was doing a rotation at the Smithsonian. Anyway, she found some document that evidently proved Darrell plagiarized a good part of his book that got him tenure. He was fired and came after Adrienne. That's why she took the job in Houston.

She'd just gotten tenure at Virginia and once again was forced to leave."

Angela choked a bit and continued. "I hoped Houston would be a new beginning for her. She deserved a break, a turn of good luck. I guess it wasn't to be."

Her voice was brusque, as if she were gathering all her emotions back under control. "I have to go. Hildy, thank you for all your help and for caring for my niece. We'll speak again soon."

I sat there staring at the phone trying to process everything I'd learned from Angela. *Did I ever really know Adrienne?* Could you really be "best friends" and have so many secrets? Could one of Adrienne's secrets have led to her death, or even to her killing Bobby Jake?

My inbox was filled with phone notes, which were easier to deal with than the jumble going through my brain. I passed the media inquiries to the team to begin calling with what little we could release. The only new information was confirmation on the identities and the time of death. I was glad to see all the new media calls were local. I also had a load of calls from friends and people across the campus.

I dialed the football office first. "Coach, I am so sorry for you and your team. How is everyone doing?"

"That's why I called. I want to arrange a campus memorial service for Bobby. It will help the team and the campus deal with this tragedy."

I could hear Coach Darrow shuffling papers as he continued. "We can use the stadium since that was a second home to him.

I'd like to do it Friday. We don't have any football games now, of course, but Coach Mickelson suggested they dedicate the rest of the basketball season to honor him. He wants to announce it at the game Saturday. I'm sure Bobby's family will want to be here for both events."

I hesitated before responding. "Both of those ideas are wonderful. But why not put them together to get the largest participation? You could do the memorial in the basketball arena before the game, and Coach Mickelson can announce the rest of the season in Bobby's honor. We'll be glad to help get the word out. Are you including Dr. Harrington in the service as well?"

Biting my lip, I knew what his answer would be.

"Well, Hildy. We were thinking about this for the athletes and helping them. And . . . well, we don't really know what happened. Under the circumstances I don't think Bobby's parents or friends would feel comfortable honoring her. You should probably look to her department to do something for Dr. Harrington."

I wasn't surprised but still could hardly keep from cursing. "Yeah, OK. I guess you're right. Once you clear this with Dr. Graves and Dr. Murphy, I'll have Stephanie on my team work with you on logistics and media announcements. Let me know when you have it scheduled."

Separate memorials? Double media insanity, sending the message that the university believed Adrienne was guilty. Maybe it was time to dig more deeply into Bobby's background.

"Hey, Coach, perhaps you can help with something else. I want to get some personal remembrances from some of Bobby's friends. We can maybe use them on the web page for the service." I was great at creating scenarios on the fly. "Can you recommend some of the players? Did he have a girlfriend or some students he studied with? Anything you can send me would really help."

"Great idea. Sure, I can ask the guys and get a list of contacts to you. I'll try to send them by this afternoon. We appreciate your help with this. I know it will mean a lot to his family and friends."

As I hung up, another idea hit for getting fast info on Bobby. Swinging around to the computer, I pulled up the class roster for the electronic news class I taught Wednesday evenings. The team needed a research project, and they could help find info on Bobby. Couldn't hurt to have them look into Adrienne's ex as well. Really, what did we know about Bobby, who he was, how he lived, what was important to him? With a thorough search of social media and talking to some of his friends, maybe we could better understand how he ended up dead on the floor of Adrienne's office.

Ten

BOBBY

Two Weeks before the Dig

"MOM. IT'S HARD ENOUGH being a junior, tripping over Dad's name on every form. But does he have to keep dragging me around like a prize bull?"

"Bobby, there's no need to be crude. Let me talk to him."

He was the golden boy. At least that's what his father always said. Senator Jake had displayed him in the Texas Senate since he was three. Dressed in a tiny suit and tie, he toddled into the chamber on his father's finger, much to the delight of the entire legislature.

Every two years, at the start of the session, the ritual was repeated. The suits getting fancier, the walk turning into a swagger. The senators less and less impressed. He still had that golden look: light brown skin, pale green eyes, curly black hair . . . the perfect result of the pairing of his Black father and his white mother. Proof of his father's egalitarian position, which allowed him to vote for his own best interests for the rest of the session.

Bobby was turning twenty that spring and refused to play the senator's game this year. He slammed into his room when he heard her solution. He'd known it was a long shot. His mother rarely went against the senator's wishes. Her plan was almost worse than the perp walk through the Texas Senate Chamber. He was not surprised his father had so readily agreed. A big blowout for his twentieth. His April birthday was in the middle of the session and a perfect break from the legislative grind. Robert Jake Sr. would invite his senate colleagues to Houston to celebrate his son's coming of age. The adult party would take place in the ballroom of their River Oaks mansion. Bobby and his friends could gather in the pool house.

Damn, I should have accepted the scholarship to Vanderbilt. But no. His father insisted if he couldn't get into Harvard or Yale, he should stay in Houston and be the big fish in the small pond. The senator's mantra . . . get great grades and extracurricular activities at a public university and parlay that into acceptance to a major law school. And he had to admit it was working. He was quarterback and junior class representative, headed for student body president next year.

But this latest trick was too much. At least he'd dodged the trip to Austin. Though he still wasn't sure it was a better deal to have all the old farts at his house where his Gulf U crew would be there to watch.

Flash responded immediately to Bobby's text. *Whasup, Bobeee?*

Flash. You have to help me. Dad is over the top . . . again. He's turning my birthday into a political rally. Meet me in the dog park. We need to talk.

Flash was from Third Ward but hung out in the upscale dog park on Allen Parkway. Bobby took his mom's Yorkie, Princess, to the same park every day. It initially got him out of the house; now it was a way to connect with Flash and a supply of oxycodone.

Flash was the wholesaler, and Bobby was one of many salesmen to high school and college students across Houston.

"Bobeee, Bobeee. Ace. Genius. I love your idea. We can make a killing with all those fat cats in one room . . . in your room. They'll be ripe. And all your fly college hotties hanging at the pool. Well, it's like a . . . smorgas . . . a buffet." Flash grinned or smirked, hard to tell with the scar cutting through his lip.

Bobby thought he looked like an African warrior with welts slicing through his cheeks and long dreadlocks tied back on his neck. His dad would go apeshit if he ever met him.

Picking up the Yorkie, Bobby walked to the gate. "Smorgasbord . . . it's smor-gas-bord. And it will be cool to use Dad's event against him. Yeah, I can see that. You're in charge of the supply. Just be careful to keep this under the radar. I want to make a big splash and break free from my family's expectations."

Flash picked up his backpack and followed Bobby up to the walking trail. "You weed out the pious ones. I'll take care of the rest. You'll have the bangest party favors ever."

His birthday wasn't for five months, and he still had the Costa Rica trip. He planned to get some new contacts while there. He might have enough of a bankroll between the two events to get his own place and make it through his senior year without flipping out. *Shit.* He was a grown man and still living at home with a pitiful allowance. He had to wait until he turned twenty-three to get access to his grandfather's trust fund. Three years. He needed the next few months to fall right, and he'd make it just fine.

Eleven

HILDY
Present

THE CAMPUS TURNED OUT in full for Bobby's memorial service. Students filled the basketball arena. During the week they had created a memorial wall on the fence around the football practice field covered in cards, flowers, and stuffed bears wearing Bobby's #11 football jersey. Tremayne's film crew was there to record every sobbing coed.

I stood in back of the stage listening to the tearful memories of his teammates, coaches, and the students who were with us in Costa Rica. All I could think of was how Adrienne was nowhere in this cathartic ceremony. No one would build her a memorial wall or weep dramatically at her service. We'd send her ashes to her aunt in Virginia to bury in the cemetery plot near her parents with little fanfare.

Earlier in the week a few of Adrienne's friends joined me in a commemorative bottle of our favorite wine and tapas. Mica and Abby came—to support me. Adrienne's colleagues all had excuses, those who bothered to RSVP. We drank three bottles of Provençal rosé, and I managed to get through it without crying or throwing my glass at the wall. My headache the next morning seemed only right.

I didn't care how many people insisted Adrienne was a murderer. It just didn't compute with what I knew of my friend. She might have had a few secrets—like her threatening ex-husband—but I could never see her as violent. Maybe if she were protecting someone. Herself? That was certainly the prevailing belief. No, I was not ready to abandon my friend. Not without proof. She was just as much a victim here as Bobby.

The question was—what could I do? If I followed my orders, and my job, I was to get the university out of the headlines. Close this down as fast as possible. Throw Adrienne under the bus. That's how I would usually handle this . . . if I weren't personally involved.

But for the first time in twenty years of closing bad stories as quickly as possible, I needed to do exactly the opposite. The longer the media hounded the story, the more time I had to find answers. As I headed home from the memorial service, my mind was racing. *I need to keep investigating while appearing to get the university out of the limelight.* Not a small task. I might need to call in reinforcements.

Shasta did her usual frenzied dance when I opened the door. Bless her heart, she'd held it for more than nine hours. I dropped my purse, grabbed her leash, and headed back out for a fast walk around the neighborhood and over to Heights Boulevard. We made it to Harvard and stopped in front of Mother's stately Victorian.

I should have known not to stand on the sidewalk staring at the mansion for too long. The double front doors opened and there she was, the grand dame of Harvard Street, or to hear her tell it, Houston. At seventy-three, she was ramrod straight. Her ash-blonde hair the same shade for thirty years, and her Donna Karan pantsuit the same size she wore as CEO of R&V Oil Services Company. She'd retired at seventy and immediately transitioned into the queen of volunteers in her second year as chair of the board of Houston Charities Foundation.

"Hildegard, are you just going to stand there and stare?" Her impervious tone hadn't changed since retiring either.

"No, Mother. I was walking Shasta and paused to admire your garden. Your guys have done their usual awesome job." My formal *mother tone* hadn't changed much in fifty years.

"Hildegard, why do you insist on using such slang? Certainly my *gardeners* have just finished with the plantings to bring in spring. A bit early, but the winter plants suffered from the mild season and were ready for the change."

Could I be less interested? On the other hand, Mother was wired into the social and political power brokers in the state. She could have insight into Senator Jake's upcoming run for governor and how Bobby's death might affect that.

"Mother, could we visit a few minutes? I'd love to get your opinion on what's happened with Adrienne and Bobby Jake." I had her with the mention of Jake, I was sure.

"Yes. Leave Shasta in the backyard with Minuit. And they better not dig up any of my plants."

We had our marching orders. Shasta would enjoy hanging with Minuit, and I would suffer tea with Mother. I entered the kitchen from the back door. Going to the pantry, I pulled out a stainless mixing bowl for Shasta's water. She'd be fine outside for an hour if necessary.

Not surprisingly, it was less than forty-five minutes when Shasta and I were back on the sidewalk, headed home.

Mother knew Cecily Jake from one of the charity balls she'd chaired in the recent past. She agreed to quietly snoop for any intel on Senator Jake and his wife and son. I was properly gobsmacked that she agreed to help. She, of course, called it *gathering intel.* Whatever worked.

I still needed to check my own sources to see how the investigation was going. I knew just where to begin.

Twelve

CHIEF WEST INSISTED WE meet off-campus at a small café miles from the university. This was not a conversation he was authorized to have with a civilian.

He glared as I approached his booth, the one furthest from the door where he could see everyone and everything going on in the café. His hands lay on the table, a mug of coffee securely within their boundaries. I sat opposite, facing him and the back wall.

"I ordered your tea," he said as the waitress approached with a mug and small pitcher of cream.

Nodding, I doctored the drink. I was in no mood for small talk, so I launched right in. "What have you found? How is the investigation going? Chief, there has to be—"

"Sorry, Hildy, but all the evidence points to her guilt." He stopped to sip his coffee, pulling back as if it burned his tongue. "They were alone in her office, and the door was locked. The dagger was Adrienne's and only had her prints—"

I interrupted, stirring my tea furiously. "Smudged. Didn't I see that on the coroner's report?" His eyebrows scrunched together.

"And yes, Chief, I got a copy of the report from the morgue. I told them I was with the university and needed it. Totally true." I received another glare. "So the perp wore gloves. And I can name dozens of locked room mysteries where someone manipulated the scene."

He jumped in before I could launch another attack. "Yes, mystery *fiction*. A neighbor identified Bobby's truck parked outside Dr. Harrington's house a few nights before the incident. Witnesses saw them having a heated discussion."

I looked up at that. The first I'd heard of any argument. Checking to ensure no one was in listening range, I asked, "Anyone hear what it was about?"

Shaking his head, West replied. "No, only the body language. The witness defined it as angry."

I jumped back in, almost cajoling. "Chief, please. I know . . . knew her. She wouldn't hurt anyone. This wasn't in her. There has to be another answer." My fingers plowed through my hair, turning it into irritated peaks. "I was with them in Costa Rica on the dig, and they were perfectly normal. No undertones. Nothing. No way did she suddenly turn murderous and kill him three weeks later."

He reached out, and I jerked back into the seat. "What? Don't pat my hand. I don't need your sympathy."

Shaking his head, he started again. "Listen. You have to leave it alone. Hell, you've already gotten a crack on your head. End this now before you really get hurt."

"Aha! So you agree with me the attack at Adrienne's house is connected to the murders." I smiled in triumph.

He almost growled. "We don't know that, but whether it is or not, take the hint. Stop this amateur meddling before you're really hurt." Looking down at his hands tightly covering the mug, he continued. "The wounds were consistent with murder-suicide. She committed the equivalent of hara-kiri when she stabbed herself in the stomach."

He evidently hoped his graphic description would scare me off.

"But—"

He held up his hand as I began to retort. "Yes, it's unusual, but I think she shocked herself when she struck him and believed death was better than prison. The dagger was the only weapon found and matched both their wounds." Stopping to take a gulp of the now cooler coffee, West continued. "She had no defensive wounds—"

"What about the bruising on her arms? The coroner noted bruises appearing a day after the murders. Someone could have held her." I'd chipped off the pink manicure from my right thumb and was unconsciously starting on the left.

"They were in a room locked from the inside. Those few bruises were most likely from Bobby. We have no witnesses, so we have to go by the evidence at the scene . . . and to the best of our ability, it leads us to murder-suicide." West leaned over the table as if daring me to continue.

I crossed my arms, pushing to the back of the booth. "You're wrong. There has to be something else. I was glad when President Murphy kept you on this case. You should be able to look beyond the obvious."

Now leaning forward, I stared at him, hoping my unwavering look would persuade him. He looked angry, barely holding onto his temper. Did he know something he wasn't sharing? Ignoring the icy coldness coming from the other side of the booth, I kept pushing.

"What about her crazy ex? He was on campus. Adrienne's aunt told me he accosted her in the parking lot. And Adrienne told me she'd threatened her chairman with an EEO suit." I barely took a breath. "Maybe Bobby was collateral damage. Or maybe he was the intended victim and Adrienne was in the wrong place. There've been rumors he was dealing oxycodone."

"Hildy, don't you think I'd know if there was a drug problem on campus? I've been doing this a long time. If Bobby was selling drugs, I would have heard about it."

"Really? OK, so maybe not a big drug ring. Do you know what every kid is up to on campus? My student reporters swear he was the go-to guy for a variety of substances to get you through finals."

"Just listen to yourself. You've spun a number of widely different scenarios, none of which you can prove. If you're even close to any of these wild fantasies, you could put yourself in real danger."

"Not a bad idea. Maybe then you'll believe there is more going on here. Someone is pulling the strings, and if I have to poke the bear to get you all looking in the right direction, well, what else can I do?"

The vein in West's neck stood out as his jaw tightened. "Stop this right now. I can't be responsible for your safety if you keep on this way. Just supposing you're right, and Bobby did have drug connections, you can't go messing around with drug dealers. And I repeat, we don't have much of that on our campus. But Houston certainly does, and people who deal drugs are fierce about protecting their turf. You have to let this go."

West waived their waitress away before she could bring the check.

I couldn't give up this last opportunity to get to him. "There are dozens of scenarios where Adrienne and Bobby are both victims. Are you even trying to track any of those down?"

West's face got even tighter. I could almost hear him grinding his teeth. He lifted his fist and looked like he wanted to slam it on the table. Instead, he carefully lowered his hand to wrap around the mug again.

"Hildy, what do you take me for? Of course we're following every thin lead. But President Murphy gave me a week to clear this before surrendering the case to HPD. I'm about to hand this over, and they are going to go with the evidence and not your Miss Marple conjectures. And Hildy, they are not going to tolerate you messing in their case. You must stop interrogating possible witnesses. You'll be charged with interfering in police business."

"I'm not interrogating. I'm just checking in with some of Bobby's friends. We were helping Coach put the memorial event together. And President Murphy was the one who asked me to talk with Angela Johnson." My knee was jiggling, a sure sign I was nervous. "Did you know Adrienne had a baby? Her aunt told me. She was just a kid. Raped. She gave it up. She never told me . . . or anyone that I know of."

West picked up his mug. It was empty, and he banged it back onto the table. "Hildy. Stop. Since you got a copy, you already know the autopsy showed she'd had a child. We are looking into all of this. Let us do our job. As much as I hate it, you and Max were right. As long as the university conducts the investigation, the media will suspect a cover-up. Do your job. Move this from the front page and let everyone get on with their lives."

After a second, I nodded, pushing my mug to the middle of the table. "I'll give them a chance, but I won't stand by and see Adrienne railroaded because it closes the case faster. I just can't do that, Chief. I can't."

That was as good as I'd give him. Pulling out his wallet, he dropped a twenty on the table. As we stood, he reached out his hand, wrapping it tightly around my upper arm to move me along. I shook loose, rubbing my arm as I walked with him out of the café.

"Look, Hildy. I know you, and you are relentless. Drop this. I'm watching you. I'll know if you continue to investigate." He sighed, taking a long breath before continuing. "And . . . if you happen to accidently discover anything . . . bring it to me. Do not tell anyone else, including your minions. I can pass it on to HPD without you being involved."

Minions? What minions? I gave him my best PR smile. Did I just get a secret hall pass? Or did he just really know me?

I was still simmering as I returned to the office. I barely got through the door before my assistant grabbed me. A call from the president did not bode well. West should have another two days to work the case. Was the university going to bring HPD in early?

I was immediately ushered into President Murphy's inner sanctum. Chief West had beaten me there. Max was scowling as only he could. A tall Black man stood staring out the window overlooking the campus. He was well over six foot tall and still had the carriage and posture of a former athlete.

"Thanks for joining us, Hildy."

President Murphy gave me his PR smile. Since I'd taught him that smile, it wasn't going to work.

"Yes sir. Of course." I PR-smiled right back.

"Hildy, Senator Jake wanted to thank you personally for helping arrange the campus memorial service for his son."

The stiff man at the window slowly turned. He didn't even offer a PR smile, just a nod.

"It was the least I could do. Senator, I met your son on the dig in Costa Rica. He was a real asset to the program, and I know his coach and teammates on the football team are missing him fiercely."

The senator fidgeted as I spoke . . . his left hand moved in his pocket as if he were fiddling with his keys or a worry stone. Maybe something of Bobby's. His dark eyes didn't land on anyone in the room. He was most likely trying to hold it together—anger, confusion, loss, regret mixed with an iron control and the privilege of his rank. None of that showed. His face looked carved from granite, lacking the usual frown and laugh lines. Would a state senator use Botox to keep his youthful appearance?

A voice from near the senator responded. "The senator's family wants to thank you and the team for all your consideration." The speaker leaned against the president's bookcase near the window in protective proximity to the senator.

The blond man, dressed in a tailored suit and what looked like Lucchese boots, continued. "Now all they want is to put all of this behind them, bury their son, and try to get on with their lives. The senator and all of us will ensure that Bobby Jr. is not forgotten. We've asked the university to turn the case over to the Houston police. Our office has always worked closely with the department. It will be best if they finish the investigation."

He looked over to the senator as he concluded, then both of the men turned again to stare out the window. Well, that certainly answered one question. I could tell West was grinding his teeth as he stared holes into the wall behind Murphy.

Examining Jake more closely with his back turned, I could tell his business suit was definitely not off-the-rack. His shoes also were high-end, perhaps hand-fashioned. State senators served for four years, meeting every other year for 140 days. They were paid a little more than $100,000 a year for their service. A great salary for a state employee, but Jake definitely was doing very well with his law practice. Both he and his chief of staff dressed in style . . . nothing off the rack. Jake's suit was some designer or other. It fit as if made specifically for him. I needed to do some research on that guy.

"Hildy."

I refocused on the president.

"Hildy. As Mr. Daniel has stated, we are transferring the case today to HPD. Please issue a press release announcing HPD will be handling the investigation as of today. All inquiries should be made to their media liaison, as your office will no longer have updated information. Mr. Daniel, as the senator's chief of staff, would like to review anything we officially issue, including your release."

Daniel glanced back. His smile didn't reach his eyes as he shifted attention from me to President Murphy. "That should free you and your staff so you can get back to your normal schedule."

All I could do was nod. Looking at the two men, I saw they appeared almost polar opposites but locked together in motivation. Jake might be really gutted by Bobby's death, but I suspected Patrik Daniel wasn't really interested in getting justice for Bobby. Could he use this to catapult the senator into the governorship? I gritted my teeth to keep from saying it aloud. If Adrienne, and even Bobby, were to get any justice, I'd have to continue my own inquiries more quietly going forward.

Chief West stood. “Thank you for the update, President. I’ll turn over my files to the HPD officer assigned to the case.”

“Thank you, Chief, for all the work you and your men have done on this. I’m sure it will be invaluable to the HPD.”

Nodding to West and then to Max and me, President Murphy dismissed us as quickly as he’d dismissed the deaths of his professor and student.

I was not ready to do the same.

Thirteen

ADRIENNE

Two Days after the Dig

THE DOORBELL RANG. SERIOUSLY? This was the first peace she'd had since squiring a dozen undergraduates on the dig in Costa Rica. She shuffled to the door in her llama slippers. Looking through the stained glass, she saw Bobby. She pulled out a key and opened the door a crack. She was in her Saturday uniform: sweats, old T-shirt, and no makeup.

"Bobby. What brings you here? How did you find my house?" She tugged the edge of her T-shirt over her sweats.

"Dr. Harrington. Sorry to disturb you at home, but I need to talk to you. It's personal."

Bobby shifted from left to right. He'd lost the bravado he'd had at the dig and looked like he hadn't slept for a while. He moved closer as if to push against the door and force it open.

Not knowing what to do, Adrienne opened the door and faced her student. "Really, Bobby. This is not appropriate. You shouldn't be here. I'll be in my office on Monday. You can come see me then."

With the door open, Bobby moved closer into her space, and Adrienne moved back a few inches.

"I just have one question. That's all. I need an answer. Then I'll go."

She glanced around the room. Her duffel still lay against the stairs unopened since she'd returned. Shrugging, she moved aside. "OK, Bobby. You're here. What do you need?"

"Are you my mother?"

Adrienne was glad her back was close to the closet door so she could lean against it for support. After a moment, she straightened her shoulders and stood to her full five feet, ten inches. She still had to look up, but she was in full professor mode.

"What the hell are you talking about? Bobby, I've met your mother. She's a wonderful woman and your biggest fan. Are you suddenly having problems at home?"

Bobby moved closer into Adrienne's personal space, looking both embarrassed and determined.

"No, no. Mom's great. Well, she's messing with my birthday, but she's OK."

Adrienne backed away, moving into her living room. "That's not for months. How could she mess with it?"

Bobby ran his hand through the tight weave of his hair.

"It's not important. I mean she's letting my dad invite his legislative friends to be part of my twentieth. He's dragged me up there since I was three. Every two years we walk into the Senate Chamber on the first day—his *legacy*, the best genes from his African American and my mother's German heritage. A lie, a twenty-year lie."

Adrienne settled on the edge of a chair. "He's proud of you, and it broadens his perspective."

Bobby's mouth twisted. "Not really. It gives him a free ride to do whatever he wants under a multicultural umbrella. Anyway, I refused to go this year, and now I have this birthday thing to deal with, on top of everything else."

He walked across the small room so he was only a foot away. Now he towered over her, but she wasn't sure she could stand again. He hesitated. "The thing is, Dr. Harrington, my dad has always pushed so much about my heritage that my friends dared me to send a DNA sample into one of those testing sites—you know, Ancestors.com."

Now Bobby was talking fast, barely breathing between words. "They sent me the results while we were on the dig. It included an ethnic analysis, countries of origin. And they matched my DNA against their database and provided a list of matches. My closest familial match was Adrienne Harrington. That would be you, right?" He'd run out of words and stared down at her.

"Bobby, I'm not the only Adrienne Harrington in the world. Besides, I'm sure those tests can show false positives." Her hands gripped the chair arm. "Have you told your parents about your concern, about the test?"

He shook his head. "Dad would explode. Mom would crater. No, you need to tell me. Did you have an affair with my father?"

"No, Bobby, absolutely not. I never had an affair with your father. I didn't meet him until I came to Houston three years ago. I lived in Virginia my whole life."

He'd dropped down to the edge of the couch, and Adrienne stood up. "Let me get you something to drink. I have some coffee, or water, maybe a soda?"

"Uh, thanks, water would be good." He was staring at his hands clasped tightly on his thighs.

"Great. I'll be right back."

Keep it together. Shit, he has my green eyes.

She finally got him out the door without revealing much. She fell back onto the couch and pulled the mug closer. Wasn't this what she'd hope for when she'd put her DNA information on Ancestors.com? It definitely fell into the *be careful what you ask for* scenario. Mica had suggested getting the DNA analysis and posting on their site. One way to reach out. Maybe the child she'd given up for adoption would also be looking. But Bobby Jake? That couldn't possibly be right. Ideas kept flashing through her brain . . . could she deny it? Bluff her way out? Admit her past? Could he really be her son?

That last question was the one that prevailed. Her mind flashed to the gang rape at the fraternity party during her junior year at Virginia. She'd gone with a friend and drank something that left her barely conscious. She'd never had sex before, and the doctors said that there had been extensive damage. No one was ever charged, and six weeks later she learned she was pregnant. She left college and gave the baby up for adoption. She'd managed to suppress most of those memories, until fifteen minutes ago.

She needed more time. This changed everything. Could the state senator have been there that night? How was he connected to the University of Virginia and that fraternity? Questions but no answers. Except perhaps to the biggest question of all. She'd wanted to know, and now, had he found her?

Fourteen

HILDY

Present

IT WAS LATE. VERY late. Classes had finally started again, and I had a lot of catching up to do. I was annoyed my watch showed it was past midnight. I was the only one in the building—even the custodial staff had finished work and headed home hours ago.

Powering down my computer, I stretched my neck from side to side to eliminate the crick that was now overwhelming. Amazing how reality rushed back in once I stopped fixating. I'd spent too many hours since work ended writing up a suspect list and adding all I'd discovered to the file. My brain was now officially fried, and it was time to shut down.

Computer off, I got to the door and realized I'd left my purse. Back into the office, I hauled my bag out of the bottom drawer. Head, shoulders, lucky they were attached. Anxious now to get home, I pulled up short as the phone rang.

Who in the hell is calling at this hour?

I knew I'd regret picking up the receiver, but it was business. There were two types of people in my opinion: those who could ignore a phone ringing and those who were physically unable to pass by a ringing phone. No guessing which type I was. *It could be a PR crisis.*

"Gulf U PR office, can I help you?"

"Back off if you know what's good for you."

"What the hell? Who are you? How did you know I was here?"

Only the static hum remained.

I'd spent the evening talking myself down from conspiracy theorizing. The police had brushed off the break-in at Adrienne's as someone taking advantage of an empty house. I took it as evidence that something more was going on. And now a threat. *Well, that does seem to add weight to my conspiracy theory.* I definitely was pushing someone's buttons. The voice was low and gravelly, but it sounded male. How did he know I'd be here at midnight? Was I being followed?

My hand started to shake as I held on to the edge of the desk. Home. I needed to get home. But was it safe to leave here by myself? Looking over to the office door, I relaxed a bit when I realized it was still locked. Call campus police. They'd provide an escort to the parking lot. Should have done that anyway, even before being scared spitless.

But would that trigger a note to Chief West? He'd already warned me about getting involved in his investigation. *I don't have much choice. Stop screwing around and call them.*

Plopping back down in my office chair, I reached again for the phone. I stared at it for a minute as if expecting it to ring and scare the shit out of me one more time. But the phone was back to being just a phone, and I dialed the five-digit internal number for security. Steadying my voice, I asked for the Wolf Pack Squad, the group of students who served as campus escorts through the night.

I agreed to stay in the office until a Wolf Pack member arrived, Dropping the phone again, I pulled out my cell.

The student escort arrived in only ten minutes. He was majoring in theater and was thrilled to tell me all about the upcoming spring play. I started breathing naturally once we reached the car. He even checked the back seat of the Subaru before I was allowed to get in and drive home. Autopilot all the way from campus to the Heights.

I kicked off my work shoes more vigorously than usual. The left one bounced off the couch after nearly killing the lamp. I'd put in a fifteen-hour day and had the heck scared out of me. *Should I call Chief West about the anonymous threat?*

I didn't need to decide because my cell phone sounded off as I finished the thought. It was at the bottom of my purse, so it had almost dropped to voice mail when I saw Chief was the caller.

"Are you wired into my brain or something, Chief?" I dropped into the nearest chair. "I think I was just about to call you."

"You think? Really, Hildy? You get a threatening call and need escort to your car, and you just *think* about calling me directly? As if I wouldn't be flagged from the monitoring system." His voice dropped. He sounded weary or just fed up. "Exactly what were you doing that late at your office, anyway. Don't you have any life? What about your dog or your mother?"

I leaned further back in the chair. For some reason, I matched my voice to his quieter inquiry. "I needed to catch up on everything. All my regular things have been on hold for a while. Time just got away from me." At least the last statement was totally true.

No fooling him. "Have you found anything new on your Adrienne research? Is it worth wearing yourself into the ground?"

"What Adrienne research? I promised to keep you in the loop if I happened to discover anything. I intend to keep that promise."

He sighed again as if speaking to a recalcitrant child. "OK. Good. Get some sleep. Last time we met, you looked *rode hard and put up wet*."

"Why, Chief, how Texan of you. I'm going to get a drink, take a hot bath, and crawl into bed. Good night. And thanks for checking on me. Hey, by the way, how did you know I got a threatening call? I didn't mention it to the Wolf Pack kid."

There was a brief pause before he answered. "Educated guess. I know you're too stubborn to call for escort unless you're spooked. And we can track incoming calls to specific lines. Your line received a call about sixty seconds before you called for an escort."

A bit 1984ish, but it worked this time. "I don't suppose you got the caller's number or can trace the call?" I could almost see his head shaking as he responded with a brief no. "Well, thanks for checking up on me, I guess." I was too tired to argue about invasion of privacy, so I hung up.

Dropping the phone on the side table, I realized I had the house to myself. Shasta was with Mother, since I had known it would be an extra-long day. She'd be fine sleeping over with Minuit. I was surprised I hadn't heard from Mother wanting an update on the case. Not wanting to jinx myself, I headed straight for the kitchen to grab the opened bottle of rosé in the wine fridge. Never got there.

Squinting as I let loose an enormous yawn, my mouth stayed open. A petite person was curled up in my spot on the sofa, her hand cushioning her blonde head. Goldilocks had come home.

I slowly lowered onto the edge of the sofa and picked up the sleeper's feet, placing them in my lap with a quick tickle.

"Yipes."

"Hey, Gracie, what are you doing on my sofa in the middle of the night, in the middle of the week?" My fingers began rubbing my daughter's foot, pushing into the arch. We both had sensitive feet and lived for a good foot rub.

Looking at her drove any leftover anxiety from the office straight out of my head. This child had all the best of my ex-husband, including his striking blond Greek god appearance. She was a pixie in size but an Amazon in spirit. Those sleepy gray eyes could focus an impenetrable beam on an interview subject, pulling out hidden secrets and details the person never intended to reveal.

Pushing hard against her arch, I dropped her foot and helped her sit up. "Don't you have a deadline tomorrow? That Pulitzer nomination won't get you off filing your piece on time."

My pride in her success was in my voice and on the walls. Over the desk hung Grace's front-page story that brought down the Smith County Commissioner and led to her job at the *Dallas Morning News.*

"That's the beauty of a blog, Mom. I can file it at three in the morning from anywhere." Matching my yawn, Grace leaned forward, wrapping her arms around me. "Jeez, Mom. Can't a girl come home to check on her mom whose best friend was just killed?"

"Thanks, kiddo . . . for coming down and for not assuming Adrienne was guilty of murder/suicide."

"Hey, I knew Adrienne too. Not as well as you, but still. Of course she wouldn't kill anybody."

Another hug, and I pulled back. "I was going to get some wine, but how about I make us hot toddies to help us sleep—and as an excuse to drink some rum on a school night. Join me?"

Grace hesitated, shaking her shoulders as if gathering her strength. "I guess that's as good a segue as I'm going to get. Love the hot tea, if its herbal. Pass on the rum. I'm pregnant . . . a little over two months, to be exact. You're going to be a grandmother sometime around the end of August or first of September."

Frozen in shock, I stared at Grace a good five seconds before reaching out and pulling her almost into my lap. "A *baby*. Really? A baby? OMG, Grace. And you're just now telling me this? How are you doing? What does your doctor say? And who's the father? Bradley? Isn't he the CNN reporter you've been seeing?"

I could barely get one question out before another was on the way. Grace sat sphinxlike as if waiting for me to wind down. "Right. To answer in order, I wanted to be sure it took before I went public . . . fine . . . textbook fine . . . and yes, Bradley . . . though he doesn't know it . . . yet."

My hand rubbed down her shoulder in an auto-soothing gesture, one I'd done thousands of times to comfort Grace after a fight with her BFFs. This was going to take a lot more than a comfort rub. "Sounds like you still have some things to work out, Gracie. What can I do to help? And what's happened now to bring you down from Dallas?"

Grace pulled the afghan over both our laps and snuggled closer. "I'm keeping her, of course." She interpreted my raised eyebrow correctly. "Yes, she's a girl until an ultrasound proves me wrong. Brad told me when we started dating that he was not the commitment type. We are great together but in a frivolous way. He doesn't want children, and I refuse to force anyone to shut down their dreams for me. I'm perfectly capable of raising this child, especially since I have the full Brentwood support system."

She fit under my arm as if she were still nine and hurting from a skinned knee.

"Sweetheart, it's not fair to him to never tell him. He has the right to make his own decision about this. Even if you don't want to get married, he should know about his daughter. You can't be sure that what he felt about the abstract idea of parenthood wouldn't evaporate in the light of his own child."

Grace mumbled in the voice she'd used as a child when caught at something. "I know you're right. Grand said the same thing."

"Your grandmother knows about your pregnancy?" I spoke carefully to keep the hurt from showing through.

"Oh yeah. We speak a couple times a week. Started during COVID so I could check in every few days, usually right after you and I talked. She's helped me think through what I want to do. And how else do you think I keep up with what's happening in the Heights and with you? She called me right away about Adrienne, which was helpful since I barely heard from you. Did you expect me to find out from a wire service feed?"

It was hard to keep from smiling. I'd created this strong, self-assured woman. Using my best Yoda voice, I responded. "*Learned you well, young Grace.* Deflection noted. And you're right, I apologize. I've been overwhelmed by everything at Gulf U. But we're talking about you. Is it really easier to talk to my mother than to me?"

"Well, jeez, Mom. Look at us. You have a closet of four-inch stilettoes that might work as lethal weapons but are ankle-breakers to wear. I'm with Sue Grafton and her belief that 'If high heels were so wonderful, men would be wearing them.' Admit it. You and

Adrienne bought those things as works of art. You didn't really wear them, at least not to work."

She looked up at me through her bangs as she did successfully since she was five years old. I'm a sucker for a cute look. "It just came out last week when I was doing my best to throw up my large intestine. Grand figured it out and told me to buy a supply of ginger ale."

My smile wobbled as I pulled my feet under my hip without letting Grace go. "Adrienne always dressed for the moment . . . GORE-TEX work boots for the dig and Louboutins for the clubs. She was fierce. You're right, I can't wear the damn things on the graveled walkways at work, but they're awesome for an evening out. Actually, I'm not sure I'll be seen in my Jimmy Choos anytime soon. I'm thinking of donating them to some foot charity. Every pair reminds me of Adrienne and my failure to prove her innocence."

Another hug, and I untangled myself. "I still need my toddy, and you need to get your sleep. You need to take care of my granddaughter, who I plan to train to call me more often than you when she grows up! Come on, let's get you settled in your room."

Looking at Grace, I noted her hesitancy. "OK, you're probably already set up at Grand's place, but she has Shasta tonight, so I get you. We can sort it all out tomorrow. I can go in late. Max will probably be relieved that I'm not bugging him about the investigation."

We walked down the hall toward Grace's room, which had changed very little since high school. Stopping at the closet, I pulled out clean linens. Turning to Grace, I touched her hand. "Adrienne had a baby while she was in college."

"She what? I never knew she had a child." Grace looked up as I closed the linen closet.

"I didn't either. She gave the baby up and just now was trying to track down her son. She talked to Mica about it." I shook my head, amazed at everyone's betrayal. "Anyway, her aunt told me she'd been raped in college, had to drop out and give the baby up for adoption."

"Wow. Look, Mom. We both have a lot to discuss, but my brain died somewhere after I got past I-45 and the 610 Loop interchange. Made it home mostly on muscle memory. Can we take this back up in the morning?"

Watching her carefully, I nodded. "I'll call Max in the morning. He'll be glad to get me out of his hair for a day. We can visit all you want then. I'll even make pancakes with blueberries like you love."

"Yum. Deal. Love you, Ma."

"Ditto, kiddo. With all my heart."

Everything seemed off the next morning. For once, Shasta wasn't poking her cold nose into my ear. The dog was still at Mother's. And Catrina, who had curled up at the end of the bed last I remembered, was not to be found either. I'd gotten to sleep in for a change, and it was already 8:30. The banging must be Grace . . . the start of breakfast.

Coffee was on and the table set by the time I showered and pulled on well-worn jeans and a T-shirt. Grace was standing over the stove as if she always flipped pancakes there, dropping bacon on the plate she handed me.

"Hey, I was supposed to cook for you." Accepting the plate, I gave her a half hug.

"No problem. The sprout is giving me heartburn currently. At least I seem to have weathered nausea. A cat was wrapped around my head like an ear-muff or something. She's a beauty. Adrienne's Russian Blue, right?"

The cat was blissing out over her food in the corner of the kitchen.

"I rescued her after everything. She gets along with Shasta, but I'm not sure I can keep her."

Grace glanced over at the cat while juggling the plate. "Ah, she's too sweet to give away. She's part of the family now. "Anyway, thanks to . . . Catrina, right? I was up early. And food actually sounded good. So I decided to make your famous blueberry pancakes. Everything was exactly where it was when I left ten years ago."

I grinned. "Not exactly the same stuff, but why mess with perfection? Besides, who has time to rearrange pots and pans?" I stopped long enough to swallow. "These are really great. Thanks, Gracie."

Grace wrinkled her nose at the old nickname as she sat down with her own plate.

I waved a piece of bacon with a smile. "Haven't had these since last time you were in town. I've missed you, my girl."

Nodding, Grace spoke quickly. "Me too. I really felt it during the pandemic, and now. Well, the baby has focused my attention on what is most important. That's why I'm moving back to Houston for a while. Grand is going to rent me her garage apartment."

My fork dripped syrup as I swung around to her. "You're moving here? That's wonderful. Great. What about your job?" I couldn't keep my voice from getting higher with each question.

Grace looked down at her plate and then back at me. "Grand and I've been talking. I'd like to be closer for her. You know she's not getting any younger. And I'd have you guys here for support during my pregnancy. The paper is fine with it since I can do my blog from anywhere and Zoom in for meetings. Mom, I really don't want to do this alone."

Getting up, I walked around and hugged her, dropping a kiss on the top of her head. "Don't take me wrong—I'm thrilled you're home. It's just all been a bit fast. I'm glad Grand has been helpful."

Trying not to sound resentful that I wasn't in the loop, I decided to take the high road. "And I love having an investigative journalist available to help me find an answer to what happened to Adrienne. How'd you like a cat? Just be sure to wear gloves when you empty the litter box. There's some parasite or something . . . toxoplasmosis, I think. Anyway, it can cause birth defects. You just need to be careful handling it."

Grace grinned with a thumbs up. "Maybe. At least she can stay with me while I'm here. I'd like that. And I'll get one of those hands-free litter boxes. I already have plastic gloves left over from the pandemic. We'll do fine. And definitely sign me up for the detective work. Let's go over to Grand's later. She has a huge whiteboard we can use for our *murder board*. If you'll bring the cat stuff, I'll introduce Catsy to her new home. I like that name much better than Catrina."

"Sounds like a plan. But I'm guessing Catrina is not going to love her cutesy new name."

The cat seemed to send her thanks as she hung over Grace's arm.

Mother agreed to let us use her Houston Charities Foundation whiteboard for our investigation. As we set it up in Grace's loft, I watched her hand rest gently on her nonexistent baby bump.

"So talk to us about my grandbaby. Do you have a doctor yet?" Mother and I both swung around to Grace.

"All's fine. My Dallas doc sent a referral after my two-month checkup. And it looks like she will be the fourth generation of Brentwood women." Her grin threatened to swallow her face.

Mother probably had images of shell pink nurseries tumbling through her brain, while visions of booties and cute caps danced through mine. Once everyone was satisfied with the murder board, we positioned ourselves around Grace's dining table. We each grabbed a hand, forming a circle. A great way to gently move into the horrible part of the day.

"Adrienne had a baby while she was in college."

Grace already had heard this, but Mother was caught cold.

"She what? I never knew she had a child." Mother sat up straight.

I nodded and continued. "I didn't either. She was raped in college and gave the baby up. Mica told me Adrienne had asked her about tracing an adoption . . . she was trying to track down her son. She might have posted her DNA on Ancestors.com. Mica had suggested that as an early attempt."

That remark pulled us back to the more urgent issue. I just stared at the whiteboard. It reminded me of an empty computer screen, waiting for the muse to speak.

After a moment, Grace picked up the marker and faced the board. She'd already unpacked her blogging set up and connected to Mother's Wi-Fi server. "OK, we begin by identifying the victims and maybe do a timeline of their day. We also list any suspects we know about and their motives, alibis, etc."

My Junior League mother was as anxious as we were to find answers and turned to me. “Do you have photos of Adrienne and Bobby?”

I opened my laptop, bringing up the Gulf U website. “I can download them from the campus site. Also Dr. Minor, Adrienne’s boss, and maybe I can pull up old records for her ex at UVA. The other persons of interest will have to have avatars for the moment.”

Grace carefully printed each name, leaving a place for more data under each one. “I know I met Adrienne a few times, but what do you know about her that could have resulted in her murder, and what have you learned so far in your inquiries?”

I didn’t answer right away. Then, my voice soft, I said, “First, I love you both for believing that she didn’t commit suicide. Put up there that she loved designer shoes . . . and her students.”

I hiccupped and swallowed a few tears. “I want us to remember her for the good things first. More seriously, a number of people had a reason to hate and/or hurt her. Her chairman, Gus Minor, hated her. He was dragging his feet about putting through her tenure packet, and she threatened him with a lawsuit. Doesn’t sound worth killing over, but it could have cost him a future deanship.”

Grace carefully wrote Gus Minor on the board with lawsuit under his name.

“A greater threat was her ex-husband, Darrell. He’s why she came to Texas. He suddenly showed up after we got back from Costa Rica. He’d hurt her before. She tried to pass it off when she mentioned it to me, but I know she was afraid of him.”

Another name for the board with “previous threat and attack” written under it.

By this time, I'd pulled up my notes and was ticking off the possibilities. "You know, it was twenty years ago, but her rape and new search for her son might have triggered something."

"Wow, Mom, what a crazy life your friend had . . . and you didn't know any of this?"

"Nope. She kept her secrets well. And I think one of them might have killed her."

Grace walked over and gave me a hug.

At that point Mother chimed in. "Hildegard, stop projecting. There were two victims here. Maybe someone was after this Bobby Jake and Adrienne got in the way. What have you learned about him?"

Opening another file, I began reading off the list. "My blogging students did some research, and I interviewed a few of Bobby's football team members. We found some interesting official and unofficial stuff. His father is a state senator and possible candidate for governor. He liked to show off his accomplished son.

"Bobby excelled at Gulf U. He had a bevy of girls following him around. You should have seen them fawning all over him at the dig. My student reporter Brit says some of the football players called them *Bobby Babes*."

Mother frowned, and Grace looked over with a grin. "That doesn't sound too deadly, unless he had a girlfriend who might have—"

I jumped in. "Possible, but my students reported that there were hints that he was the go-to guy for drugs to get through finals and other needs, which could have proved more dangerous."

Nodding, Grace noted that on the board. "Yeah, maybe a drug deal went bad or he tried to cheat his dealer." Turning to me, she spoke quietly. "Mom, we have to look at the other possibility. Could Adrienne have had a thing for Bobby? Did you notice anything strange in Costa Rica?"

Shaking my head vigorously, I stood up and paced across the room. "No, nothing seemed out of order in camp, at least not between those two. Actually, I did wonder about Bobby's relationship with Jack Tremayne. They seemed very familiar with each other, although not exactly friendly. Bobby seemed to be avoiding the reporter, which was unusual since he was a camera hog usually, star quarterback and all. Tremayne seemed to find it very amusing. He also was his usual smarmy self with the coeds . . . and I think Adrienne had an uncomfortable encounter with him before the dig. Put him on the board. I love seeing him as a suspect."

Mother's perfect nails tapped against the marble countertop. By this time, we'd moved to the kitchen's center island as our gathering space. "If there was nothing between Adrienne and Bobby, why were they in her office together? No classes scheduled. Didn't you tell me Chief West said there was some kind of argument between them at her home? Her neighbors reported his car there earlier that week. Something had to be going on." Mother folded her arms and waited as if I had all the answers.

I walked to the board and stared at the pictures of my friend and her student. My finger lightly traced around their faces. "No, that would be too weird," I whispered.

"What? Speak up, Mom. What do you see?"

Stepping back, I picked up my reading glasses from the table and then squinted at the board. "I don't know. It's just I never really looked at them next to each other. Do you see something in the eyes? The shape, the color?"

Taking my glasses off, I rubbed my eyes. "I must be getting tired and seeing things. Just a trick of the photo or something that their eyes look so similar. Let's stop for an early supper. I think I've fried my brain."

Fifteen

THE PHONE MESSAGES STACKED on my desk were sending me a reproachful vibe. I never failed to return a call within twenty-four hours, and it had been two days. Sure, there was a weekend in there, but did anybody really care about time off anymore?

It had been a great weekend with all three generations of Brentwood women together. Grace and Mother were bonding over cooking lessons, so everyone ate well, and all Grace's boxes got unpacked. I was amazed to make it through two days without Mother driving me over the edge.

Back to reality. Right on top, as if glaring at me, was a message from Jack Tremayne. I also had five texts and four emails with his name on them in my cell. Maybe I could interrogate him while he was trying to get information from me.

I still had his private number from when we were setting up the shoot at the dig. It rang three times, and I was preparing to leave a voice mail when I heard a breathless "Hello."

"Jack? This is Hildy at Gulf U. I'm sorry for the delay in getting back to you. I've been swamped, as you can imagine. I'll be happy to visit with you. How about meeting at Martha Blue's? It's quiet and they have great cappuccino."

I hardly took a breath and left him no time to comment or beg off. "Great, no objection? I'll meet you there right after work . . . about six. Thanks, see you then."

Amazing, he hadn't had a chance to say a thing. Very unusual for Jack Tremayne—or any reporter, for that matter. I was on a roll. Surely there was someone I could interview before the day ended. Gus Minor. If he was in his office, I could go there under the guise of getting the department involved in a memorial for Adrienne.

Classes were starting, and the quad was busy with students moving into the dorms. Faculty bustled to the library to complete their research as they were confronted with sixty or more students.

Houston was having a mild midwinter day, and the walk from the Akers building to social sciences was unusually pleasant. But I wasn't fooled by the seventy degrees. It was still six weeks before the rodeo. Everyone knew Houston's winter wasn't over until after the rodeo parade, where it was always cold and rainy.

But today I enjoyed the unseasonable warmth and no humidity. I made it to Minor's office in a comfortable fifteen minutes. Knocking on his doorjamb, I stuck my head in.

"Dr. Minor. Got a minute?" When he nodded without looking up, I moved into the unusually spacious office. He had a great view of the fountain and statue. "I just wanted to check in with you. Any concerns from your faculty? I see the police have removed the crime tape from Adrienne's office, so that should help morale a bit . . . no longer an active crime scene and all."

Minor responded in his usual taciturn style. "Fine. Everyone's fine. Glad the tape is gone. Fine otherwise."

I needed my stellar interview skills to get much out of the department head. "That's good. I also wanted to see if you'd thought any more about what the department wanted to do to celebrate Dr. Harrington's life?" I'd never heard an actual harrumph before.

He looked up from the folder on his desk and glared. "No, no department function. Not up to me. If someone wants to, fine."

I tried one last push. "OK, I know you weren't close. She threatened to sue you, if I heard right. That could have ruined your chances for the deanship when Dr. Clark retires. I can't imagine how mad you must have been."

Minor wiped his hand over his nearly bald head, and his eyes squinted even tighter. His face was turning an interesting shade of puce. "I can't talk about personnel issues. Didn't with the police. Won't with you. They will have to get a warrant. You get a *no comment*."

Backing out of the room, I nodded. "Right. Well, thanks for your time. I'll keep you posted on the plans."

No reply expected. Walking back to the elevator, I had to pass Adrienne's office. Could the overweight professor have the wherewithal to commit two violent murders? Would he kill to keep his job? Shaking my head, I didn't think I'd learned anything from that confrontation. Hopefully, he wouldn't be mad enough to report me for questioning him. Could there be anything in Adrienne's office? And who knew the credit card in the doorjamb would work on the flimsy office locks? Pushing the door, I said a prayer to the lubrication gods that the hinges were well-oiled.

I slipped in and was overwhelmed by Adrienne. Her most prized possessions were on the shelves in the tiny space. Her teaching award from her first year at Gulf U. Her book on the slave trade in Central America, which she'd submitted for tenure. Shards of pottery sat alongside an intricately painted bowl with a crocodile design in red and black. Adrienne said this bowl dated from the first century . . . two thousand years old. *I need to get that to Adrienne's aunt Angela.* What I wanted would be a bit more current. A diary or notes from the dig. Inspecting the papers still on the desk, I tried to keep the fingerprint dust from messing my winter white sweater. The police had been through all this stuff, but my knowledge of Adrienne might uncover something. At the bottom of the trashcan was an envelope from Ancestors.com.

Mica said she mentioned that site to Adrienne when they were discussing her missing child. Had she followed through and sent her DNA into Ancestors to match it with other customers' DNA? They must notify people of any matches that are made.

Damn. What if my wild-haired idea yesterday had a kernel of truth? Could there be a family link between Adrienne and Bobby? Do such life-changing coincidences really occur? I folded the envelope and slipped it in my purse. I kept trying to make sense of all the strings. Taking a deep breath, I decided to worry about the truth behind the envelope once I got home. I made a note in my phone to ensure President Murphy ordered Adrienne's personal stuff be sent to Angela Johnson.

I opened the door, looking both ways. Coast clear, I slipped out, automatically pushing the lock. After a few steps, I looked back at the door. Well, damn. Not all that hard to end up with a locked room after all.

I was marking off people of interest, and Jack Tremayne was next on the list. Grace had agreed to do the online search on the entire list for background. She even thought she could tap into the *Morning News* database to get any financial information on them, particularly on Tremayne and Senator Jake.

Before I confronted Tremayne, I needed a full picture of his past. There were rumors he'd had run-ins with some less-than-reputable folks in town. The station blew it off as *the cost of getting the stories*, resulting in their most recent local Emmy award. Was it more?

I was home in record time. In some ways, I missed the days of working at home and connecting by Zoom rather than making this commute . . . the only positive note from the pandemic. I marched into the house, ready for action.

Reaching down, I gave Shasta a perfunctory pat as she spun around to welcome me home. "Good girl. Glad to see you too. No need to try to guilt me for leaving you this morning. I know Grace took you out at least twice and gave you more treats than you'd get from me."

Shasta always made me smile. She was the best roommate I'd ever had, though Grace was a close second.

"Hey, Grace. I'm home, if you couldn't tell from the wildly wiggling—"

Grace interrupted. "Mom. Great. Can you come back here? I've found some stuff."

My forward motion was hampered by a lithe gray feline winding around my ankles. "I see you brought Catsy back. I'll be there as soon as I can keep from tripping over small animals."

Grace's new apartment was being painted, so she was with me for a few days. She had her laptop set up next to mine on a small desk overlooking the back deck. Three fountains gurgled a watery welcome to the doves and neighboring jays.

Ignoring nature, Grace had her eyes locked on the spreadsheet she was creating. "OK, Mom. I've taken the information your students gathered and did a deeper background search. So far, your Dr. Minor has been cited three times for harassment, including a formal EEO bias complaint from female faculty—"

I interrupted the data dump with a vehement nod. "Got that right. He treats women faculty, and the rest of us, as servants . . . and not very bright ones at that."

Grace continued, unfazed by my interjections. "None of the charges were ever proven. He's definitely vulnerable if Adrienne had launched her suit. But other than being a Neanderthal, I didn't find much. No major conflicts, arrests, or convictions, and no other apparent source of income except the university."

Looking over her shoulder, I finished the thought. "So, if Adrienne had filed and won, he might have lost his administrative job but not his tenured position. He'd still have a job. Would that be worth killing for?"

Tapping the keys to pull up another record, Grace continued. "Now, if we look at Jack Tremayne, the picture is much more complicated. He doesn't have an overt reason for killing either Adrienne or Bobby." Pausing for a second to push her bangs out of her eyes, Grace went on. "But there is plenty of murky stuff in his background, including spending way beyond his official salary from KRVU. His tax forms list 'consulting' as the source of the bulk of the other income."

I rubbed my eyes, tired of staring at the small text on the computer screen. Giving Grace a half hug, I stepped away to the massage chair that held the primo place in the office. I raised the footrest, and both animals jumped into my lap, curling around each other for the best nap place.

"My new normal." I laughed and ruffled the gray and white coats. I spoke under my breath, just musing. "I wonder if KRVU is aware that their full-time reporter is earning so much outside of their purview? And what the hell would he be consulting on . . . how to smile without getting laugh lines? The art of hitting on young girls?"

Time to ask him and see where that went.

Sixteen

ADRIENNE

One Week before the Dig

OPENING ONE EYE, ADRIENNE recognized the mural she'd painted on her living room ceiling.

Home, she thought. *Thank God. Feel like holy hell.*

She raised her head enough to sight down her body. Fully clothed. Well, except for the blouse partly buttoned . . . but her slacks were still zipped.

A déjà vu moment sent her back twenty years, waking up in her dorm a disheveled mess and sore everywhere. Blood. She had blood on her shirt and pants, with no memory of what had happened. She remembered the dryness in her mouth, the fuzziness in her brain . . . the horror of not knowing and the fear of remembering.

The heavy weight on her chest wasn't the beginnings of a heart attack. Her ten-pound Russian Blue, Catrina, was draped across her upper chest. She moved the cat and tried to sit up.

Think. She'd changed after work to meet Jack Tremayne . . . at that French bistro. He was charming. It wasn't a real date, but she hadn't felt so hot for a man in a long time. She'd friend-dated a few times but no one serious since coming to Houston and escaping her dangerous ex.

Maybe her libido was waiting to let loose. The last she remembered was feeling woozy after drinking the wine.

Pulling Catrina back into her lap, she hugged her close. Her mind reeled. *Tremayne. He brought me home. Did I ask him in? I never bring men here.*

An empty bottle of cabernet lay on its side on the coffee table next to two stemless wine glasses. They'd evidently had more wine. No wonder she felt so odd, her mouth so dry. But why the déjà vu moment to the rape so long ago?

Adrienne tried to stand and nearly tripped. She was wearing only one of her red Jimmy Choos. Kicking off the three-inch heel, she picked up the empty bottle and glasses and placed them on the granite pass-through to the kitchen as gently as possible—no breakage, no loud sound.

Looking around, she noted the red pillows on the gray leather sofa. The Native American jug on the bookcase was in its place. As far as she could see, nothing was broken. Maybe nothing happened. She found herself rubbing her left wrist. A purple bruise was beginning to form . . . almost in the shape of a hand. She shuddered.

Shower. She needed to shower for about an hour. Her mind was sputtering, dragging through parts of last night and racing through worries about today. She was talking to herself or the cat. "Hildy will go nuclear if she thinks Tremayne hurt me in any way. At the very least, she'd demand the station pull him from the shoot."

As much as she'd like never to see Tremayne again, Adrienne couldn't prove he'd done anything to her . . . and she didn't need the negative publicity. *Hell, I'll come off as promiscuous and whiny, sleeping with someone on a first date and then bitching about it.*

Who'd believe the much-honored newscaster had to resort to drugging his dates. The scandal would be just what Minor needs to finally deny my tenure.

She didn't wait for her cat to agree. She knew what she had to do—act as if nothing had happened.

"Don't ask, don't tell."

Seventeen

HILDY

Present

I TRACKED TREMAYNE TO the old editing suite at KRVU. I knocked on the door, and he shot out of his chair. No one was supposed to be in this part of the station. After the tech upgrade, these booths were being decommissioned and donated to Gulf U. I'd toured them a few weeks before to assign the donation.

"What are you doing here? How the hell did you get past security?" It would be hard for him to sound any less welcoming. "How did you even find us?"

I hesitated a second before answering. Moving just inside the door, I leaned back against the frame. "I thought we were meeting at Martha's Blues to catch up. When you didn't show, I tracked you down. The guy on the desk told me you and Edgar were in the old editing room." Looking at the screen, I continued. "I'm responding to your earlier call. Checking in. Any new information on Adrienne and Bobby's deaths?"

Tremayne turned all the way around to look directly at me. "Other than the transfer of the case to HPD, they aren't giving us anything new. I'm going over the tape from Costa Rica. I'm betting I can find something that shows they were having an affair."

"That's a lie." My voice was low.

Swiveling back around to the editing board, Tremayne responded. "Can't prove it one way or another. Anyway, I can use some of these scenes to move the viewer in that direction."

I walked further into the editing booth and grabbed his arm, pulling him around.

Edgar turned as well. Shaking his head, he reset his earphones and returned to the screen he was reviewing. His movement dragged my attention to the computer, and I let Tremayne go. There was Adrienne being interviewed at the dig site in Costa Rica.

We both stared at her image. Jack looked like he was holding something back. I remembered their interaction on the dig. Adrienne had avoided him. Something must have happened during his "preinterview." There was a strange encounter right as they began filming.

Adrienne stood toe-to-toe with him, waving her arms. "Keep your slimy hands away from Brianna." Tremayne was about to give the young coed an open bottle of water. "What's in that water? Don't you dare try to drug one of my students. I'll have you brought up on charges." Adrienne's voice was shrill, and Tremayne looked livid.

He dropped the bottle and threw up his hands. "Hey, it's just water. Are you crazy? Calm down." They both walked away, but it must have been more than just a misunderstanding.

Looking away from the video screen, Tremayne stared at me.

He's worried I overheard the fight or that Adrienne had confided in me. I wish she had.

"OK, Hildy, what really brings you down here to the bowels of KRVU after work hours?" Jack pushed his chair back to the editing board and signaled Edgar to keep rolling the tape.

My eyes stayed on the screen as I spoke. "Well, Jack, just wondering how close you were to Adrienne . . . and Bobby, for that matter. That looked like a pretty heated discussion you had with Adrienne. She pushed you away . . . made you drop a bottle of water that splashed all over your shoes."

He grimaced. They were probably $1,500 boots. "Not sure what you thought you saw. Here's all the footage . . . no great brouhaha with Adrienne."

I shook my head and smiled. "I suppose not, after you guys have been in here editing it all. So, then, how about Bobby? I didn't think you had ever met him—"

"Not that I remember," Tremayne broke in.

My smile widened. "Then what were you two talking about right after you got on-site . . . in the middle of the night? You were just a few feet from my tent and woke me with your whispering. Sure sounded like you were well-acquainted and not all that happy about something."

Tremayne pushed back and stood up, herding me toward the door. "Dreaming. You must have been dreaming. I met the kid there on the dig. I interviewed him, and that was all." He tried to keep his voice steady. "Now you have to leave. I have work to do, and unauthorized people are not allowed down here."

Giving up for the moment, I turned toward the door. "We aren't finished with this, Jack. Something was going on. I'll find it. I won't stand for Adrienne taking the fall."

The door was on a hydraulic latch and slowly closed, though it would have felt good to slam it.

I was not finished with this. Not at all.

Eighteen

TREMAYNE

Present

TREMAYNE SAT BACK DOWN in the editing booth and looked over Edgar's shoulder. His eyes shifted to the left, where he could see himself in the reflection of one of the computer screens. He smoothed his hand across his professionally cut brown hair. Nothing out of place. He wouldn't let that PR bitch get in his head, shake his confidence. This was his ticket to the big time. He just had to wield it right. His attention was pulled back to the editing screen as the video rolled of his arrival at the dig in Costa Rica.

"Edgar, pull in on me as I get out of the copter. But cut that shot where my hair is blowing all to hell. Can't you tweak the video to get past the wind?"

The editor gritted his teeth and kept working the board. He had already edited this video into a decent three-minute feature. In the normal world, it should have been relegated to the old news file.

But now that the story was tied to two deaths, it was a possible star-maker. Tremayne was demanding a new five-minute clip he could pitch to the network and add to his clip reel.

"There, that's the shot. The cute blonde in the khaki shorts and bandana top. She's showing me the spoon she found. Can you believe the university paid that professor to take those kids to Costa Rica to find old spoons? Your tax dollars at work. Lucky for me she managed to get herself killed, making this a very valuable interview."

Tremayne nodded at his screen self as he watched the brief interview with Adrienne. "Oh, here. Grab this bit with the kid, Bobby." He leaned back and said, more to himself than his editor, "Cocky little punk but good-looking. A paler version of his father . . . in more ways than one."

As the editor continued rolling through the shots, Tremayne imagined going live on CBS Evening News. He was prepared to announce the murderer of the gifted student and his lovely professor. So which would be better? Ratings heaven . . . or the $20,000 he could get by withholding what he knew?

The dark editing booth faded into the background along with the low buzz of electronics and the hazy glow of the two screens. Tremayne saw himself in full makeup and his new charcoal light wool suit, silver-gray shirt, and red tie . . . his power look. He was seated next to the Evening News anchor, breaking the story to the world. Hell, he could get his money and then go national. What could the guy do? He'd be in jail, and no one would believe him if he yelled extortion. This could be the most lucrative deal he'd ever put through.

They say timing is everything. His random stroll across the Gulf U campus last week was going to pay off. He'd wondered what the guy was doing, so he followed him to the professor's office. The man's furtive movements triggered Tremayne's journalistic gut. He'd taped it all on his phone. All he had to do was play back the crucial seconds to make his point.

Tremayne's laugh broke into Edgar's concentration.

"What's so funny?" He looked at Tremayne and then back to the screen where he was skimming through B-roll shots of the camp.

"Life. Luck." Tremayne was back in the dark room, facing the flickering computer. "We need to get this finished. I have things to do."

Edgar scowled at the royal *we* and returned to manipulating the knobs and sliding the controls. "Give *me* another five minutes, and you can have this."

Tremayne cringed at the seedy look of the bar. He'd had to Google and relied on his GPS to find it. After an agonizing drive, all doors securely locked, he'd ended up at the docks near the ship channel. He expected to see brawny stevedores leaning on the bar. He hadn't covered this part of town since his rookie days. As he walked in, he checked himself automatically in the grimy glass of the door, an action that would register only if anything had been out of place.

He should have been home with a beer, watching the Rockets. Edgar had finally finished his brilliant demo reel, and it was ready for the network. He was due a bit of respite, especially after the run-in with Hildy. What the hell was she doing sticking her nose in? The case was out of the university's hands. HPD was in charge. She didn't have anything on him. She couldn't.

His phone erupted with Queen's "We Are the Champions," and he practically threw it at the wall before answering. *Why did I agree to this meeting? He's not calling the shots. I'm in charge here.*

Tremayne mumbled to himself, drawing the notice of the scruffy drinker closest to the door. Wiping his hands, he moved to the booth in the back of the bar. He figured he'd arrived first, so he sat facing the door, waiting for his mark. He'd stopped at the bar long enough to order a bottled beer. Taking a drink, he looked up to see one of the nondescript denizens coming over. He slipped into the booth across from Tremayne, placing his draft beer on the scarred wood.

"Sorry, I'm waiting—oh, it's you." Tremayne grinned, looking at the bum. "That's a new look for you . . . I kinda like you in rags."

Taking a long drink from the mug, the man narrowed his eyes. "And you look a bit out of place in your tie."

Tremayne looked down at his sports coat and button-down shirt. "I'm a journalist and can go anywhere like this." This was no friend, more a client. Jack had information and would provide it for a price. He was equally happy to keep the information he had on this client from going anywhere else. A win/win. "So do you have it? I still don't know why we had to do this in person, but whatever. Hand it over."

A thick manila envelope appeared on the table and was pushed across. Tremayne pulled a memory stick from his pocket and dropped it on the table.

Tremayne opened the envelope to ensure it held what he expected. "Good. I don't suppose I need to count it. Do you need to check the footage?" At the shake of his head, Tremayne continued, "OK, then. This will do for now. Not that I don't love the atmosphere, but I think our business is done here."

"Yes, it most definitely is." The grubby man's comment didn't really seem addressed to Tremayne but more a general announcement. He stood and leaned in. One hand wrapped around the envelope on the table, and the other held a thin knife, which quickly disappeared into Tremayne's chest.

As the reporter slumped, the man patted him on the shoulder. "Now we're done."

Nineteen

HILDY

Present

MY KNEE KEPT JITTERING as I waited outside the president's office. I'd slept less than four hours. But hey, that was the most I'd had all week. A blood test would show my caffeine content at over 50 percent.

Grace was settled back in Mother's garage apartment after a full day of conspiracy theorizing and ice cream devouring. Max had been glad to have me out of the office for a while. But now I was back to reality, my worst nightmare . . . the offline investigation into the deaths had surfaced. It would have been worth it if I'd found anything to change the murder-suicide verdict of the police. But so far, nothing. I didn't care. My gut still screamed that Adrienne was not a murderer. And I was sure Tremayne was hiding something—I just didn't know what. Yet.

At the buzzer, the secretary looked up. "The president is ready for you now, Ms. Brentwood. You can go right in."

Nodding, I pushed up from the low chair and walked slowly to the glass door with the Gulf State University seal etched in the center. Inside, Max and President Murphy waited. An HPD detective stood over to the side, at parade rest, her feet shoulder length apart, her arms clasped behind her back. All three stared at the door as I made my way into the inner sanctum.

Dr. Murphy spoke first. "Sit, please, Hildy, sit. We just need to clear a few things up. Detective Strand here says a number of her witnesses reported speaking with you over the past few weeks. They thought you were part of the investigation, even after it was passed from Chief West to the Houston police. I also have a report that some of our students were involved with you in this pursuit."

His stare was the one I'd seen only when he was focused on a student who had acted out. First time it was leveled at me, and I gave it full credit for invoking a sense of guilt.

He continued, "I'm sure they must have misunderstood, as this is no longer a university issue. And I'm sure you would never involve your students in anything outside of your duties to Gulf State University."

My damn knee was jittering again as I tried to explain. "There were just some inconsistencies . . . questions came up that needed to be answered." I fumbled for the right words. "My students were working on their research skills using a true-life event to delve into database studies. They were never in touch with anyone directly."

Detective Strand looked about to jump in when Max Levine cut her off. "You went against my direct orders to stay away from the Harrington-Jake investigation. You are not a naive employee. You knew you were skirting the line and crossing it more often than not."

I mentally took the fifth. Max's look of disappointment was almost worse than the president's glare as he spoke with all his authority.

"I know that you and Dr. Harrington were close, and this has been hard on you and her friends. But this ends here." Leaning over his desk, President Murphy spoke slowly. "Let me be perfectly clear about what happens next. Ms. Brentwood, you are to immediately cease any and all efforts you or any of your students are doing that infringe in even the smallest way on Detective Strand's case. I don't want to hear a whisper of a rumor that you are continuing your amateur detective work. It is dangerous for you and your students. Any violation of this directive will result in disciplinary action up to and including dismissal for insubordination. Do I make myself clear?"

My reporter instincts were ready to yell; however, self-preservation won. I just nodded without speaking.

President Murphy stared, waiting for a verbal agreement.

Finally I spoke. "I understand and apologize, Detective Strand, if I have impeded your investigation in any way."

At least it sounded like the detective was still investigating. That was something, anyway.

It was only 3:30, but I just couldn't face pitiful looks from my staff and colleagues. They, of course, knew where I'd been, and President Murphy's ultimatum would be across the campus by now. I stopped at the office only long enough to grab my laptop and tell Amy to forward emergency calls only.

Twenty minutes later, I was back in my driveway, staring out the windshield at the garden gate and the blue art glass lantern. No blinding flashes of brilliance, just cedar planks. Could I trust that Detective Strand would find the truth? It looked like the officer was happy to take the easy way out, though her pushback might mean she was still investigating.

Unsnapping the seat belt, I got out and headed for the house. Shasta was yapping at the door, her excitement bringing a reluctant smile. I could always count on my favorite cheerleader for a happy moment. And there was Grace, at Mother's with a new baby on the way. Hell, I had a basketful of good I should be celebrating.

Maybe they were right and there was nothing to find, just wisps of fog. Everything still pointed to Adrienne killing Bobby and herself. Despite all my digging, I hadn't found anything to prove otherwise. Maybe that was because there was no proof and Adrienne really did it.

Shasta showed her gratitude for her mom's early arrival by pawing at my knee and wiggling across the room. Leaning down, I gave her a quick belly rub and snapped the leash on for a walk. Ten minutes later, we were back and ready to cuddle on the couch. I didn't want to see anyone or do anything for the rest of the day. Mindless television. I clicked the control, and KRVU's afternoon game show blared on. Before I could switch the channel, the *Breaking News Bulletin* flashed on the screen.

The twenty-something afternoon anchor looked flushed. "One of the most beloved members of our news team has been found dead. Emmy-nominated investigative reporter Jack Tremayne has been identified as the body found stabbed last night in a bar near the ship channel. HPD is investigating this as a homicide. So far, there are no suspects, and police sources say they are looking at Tremayne's ongoing investigations." The newscaster blinked back what appeared to be real tears. "We will keep our viewers informed of any breaks in the case. A special memorial service will be scheduled in the next week and broadcast live here on KRVU."

The news bulletin flag was replaced with a sign that the station was now returning to regular programming.

I stared at the screen, not seeing the smiling host or the greedy game show players. Clicking the power button, I dropped the remote in my lap. I'd hated Tremayne as the epitome of bad journalists and as a grubby human being. Young female reporters across the city would now be safe from his wandering hands. So why feel so bad? Someone had destroyed my nemesis but also my prime suspect. Could it be connected? How could it not? Everyone believed my attack at Adrienne's house was a coincidence. Surely they'd see this new murder as proof that something was going on beyond Adrienne and Bobby.

I grabbed my phone and dialed Grace. "Have you heard?"

"Mom, hello. And if you mean the rumbles from the campus about you being chewed out by President Murphy, then no, but I'd love to hear —"

Shaking my head vigorously, I interrupted. "Oh, that's old news. No. Jack Tremayne's been murdered. They found his body in some seedy bar. It has to be linked to Adrienne. He knew something, and it got him killed. I'm coming over. Call Mother. We need to go over the information on all the suspects. Someone is getting nervous."

Grace was sputtering as I clicked the end button.

It didn't matter how many cases or enemies Tremayne had. His death proved Adrienne was murdered. All I needed to figure out was what the reporter knew that got him killed.

Twenty

THE THREE-STORY VICTORIAN was as pristine as when she first graced the boulevard in 1910. As usual, I took a moment to admire the workmanship. It was on the National Register of Historic Places, and deservedly so. My old bedroom was in the turret on the third floor, which was a princess's castle, Rapunzel's tower, or a mountain hideout, depending on my imagination.

Mother had turned the old garage into an office and small apartment, and Grace had officially moved her stuff in. I decided she planned on staying awhile, since it was beginning to have her personal stamp. At nearly thirty, Grace embodied the straightforward, work-driven ethos that translated into leather, glass, metal furnishings, open-concept layout (whatever happened to walls and rooms?), stainless appliances, and concrete floors and countertops. Not quite minimalist but bordering on it.

Mother's garage apartment was perfect for the moment—close enough to get baby help and removed enough to reject it if the advice got too intrusive. Of course, it wasn't her forever home, but it was perfect for transition to motherhood. Looking at her new space, I decided Grace had absorbed some wildness from me—through osmosis, no doubt. Her leather translated into chili pepper red and turquoise—couch and reading chair. Her metal was twisted, more black wrought iron than chrome. And she favored the kaleidoscopic hues of stained glass over tempered. In defiance, or more probably, to mark her space, Grace already had placed a large red Japanese pot next to the stairs leading to her loft. In a month or so, the hibiscus it held would have yellow flowers the size of salad plates.

With her limited furniture and wide-open space, Grace's loft (OK, not very lofty on the second floor of a garage) also served as our headquarters for any off-the-books research we needed to conduct. We dragged out the murder board we'd created a few evenings before. Photos of the victims and persons of interest were fixed across the top with lines making connections and keywords beneath each.

Jack Tremayne's publicity headshot was center stage. He was my favorite villain candidate from the beginning, probably because he was such a pain. He now had to move to the victim side of the board. Under his photo, I wrote: "Blackmail? Connection to Senator Jake . . . Bobby? Meeting with Adrienne? Argument at dig?"

Grace walked in as I was erasing Tremayne's earlier list of connections and writing the new ones. Many of the words that suggested he was the killer also described why he was now a victim.

"You know, Mom, this still doesn't prove that Adrienne was an innocent victim." Grace stood back, her hand resting on her slightly rounded belly as she stared at the full board. "It's all circumstantial. If he was really a blackmailer—"

"What do you mean *if*?" Turning from the board, I stabbed the marker toward her.

Grace grabbed hold of it. "Don't point that loaded marker at me. I'm on your side. I agree there could be a case for blackmail based on his financial records. Even so, it looks like he's been at this for a while. There are no doubt lots of people who are happy he is no longer around. His death could have nothing to do with Adrienne or Bobby."

Without a good answer, I turned back to the board, drawing a line from the photo to a printout of an Excel spreadsheet. "I appreciate you tapping into the *Morning News* system. I didn't realize you had access to people's banking information."

Grace sat at her desk and pulled up the file on her computer. "We don't, actually, but one of the business reporters tracked this down a few months ago when doing a listing of the top-paid broadcasters in the state. Tremayne came in close to the top, which was interesting since he wasn't an anchor. I thought it was odd at the time."

I moved behind her to read off the screen. "Five thousand dollars every month like clockwork, and then another seventy-five hundred every six weeks or so. He was more than doubling his income somehow. And blackmail fits the bill."

Grace tapped her fingers on the desk. "So, if you're right, Mom, what information did Tremayne have against Adrienne or Bobby or even Senator Jake? He's been preying on somebody for a while, so was he killed for that or for knowing something about Adrienne's death . . . and how are we going to prove it? Based on what I heard about your run-in with President Murphy, how do you plan to do this without getting fired?"

Putting down the marker, I began to rub her shoulder. "Carefully. Very carefully."

"Chief, you've got to believe me now. Tremayne was up to his eyeballs in what happened to Adrienne and Bobby, and it got him killed." My words shot out as if from a revolver, taking a huge gulp of air as I wound down. "His bank records show regular deposits of large sums outside of his KRVU payroll." I hated doing this over the phone . . . I couldn't get a handle on his reaction. I'd just texted him a copy of the spreadsheet with Tremayne's past year's income.

Waiting was never my strong suit. I imagined West rubbing his hand across his scalp, his usual sign of frustration. "Hildy, you are going to get fired . . . or worse . . . if you don't let this go. Why call me, anyway? I've nothing to do with the investigation."

"Listen. Just listen. Tremayne knew something. I felt it last time I saw him. We had words in his studio where he was messing with the video from the dig." I sat up straighter, looking over at the murder board. "He could have confronted the killer, demanding money for silence. You know, when he saw Bobby in Costa Rica, I swear he already knew him. He asked about 'the old man.' That had to be the senator. He was making a point, a connection."

I no longer could sit still and began meandering around the room, still speaking into the phone now resting on the table's edge. "Tremayne knew things about people. I bet he knew lots of damaging things. What if he padded his income by selling that information to interested third parties—or more likely by blackmailing people to keep from going public with it. He knew something about Senator Jake. I'd bet my life on it."

The No. 2 pencil in the cup next to the phone found its way into my mouth, and I bit into the eraser. Gnawing through the rubber, I spit the small red blob onto the table.

"Sit down, Hildy. Stop pacing and put the pencil back in the cup."

Did he have a camera in Mother's garage apartment? How'd he do that?

West continued. "You're right. Tremayne was in a position to know lots of secrets from lots of important people. If he was blackmailing them—and I won't ask how you got his bank records—what makes you think it has anything to do with Adrienne's death? Any one of his victims might have wanted to stop—"

My frustration gushed through the phone as I cut him off. "Timing. Look at the timing. I start pushing him and others. I get attacked in Adrienne's garage, and now Tremayne is killed. I don't believe in coincidences. These are linked. I know it."

West's deep sigh came through the iPhone speaker as clearly as if he stood in the room. "HPD isn't going to see it that way. There is less to connect Tremayne's murder to Adrienne's than there was with the attack on you. Neither is proof that she did not commit murder and suicide."

Before I could launch another foray, he pushed through. "And what if you're right? You've painted a huge target in the middle of your back. The least of your problems is getting fired. You're going to get yourself killed." His voice softened. "Please, Hildy, back away. HPD will look into Tremayne's income as standard procedure. You need to stop. Your job is to get the university out of the spotlight on this, not to be the one holding the torch. Let the Houston police do their job. They haven't closed either case. They're still investigating every possibility."

I couldn't believe I'd held out any hope for his support. Nonetheless, I refused to let him wave me off. "Right, Chief. Sure. Thanks for listening to my ravings. I'll be back in the office tomorrow if you need anything." I hit end before he could reply.

Twenty-One

ADRIENNE

Two Days before Her Death

ADRIENNE WAS ENJOYING HER solitude. The seven-story building was almost empty. Classes wouldn't start for a few more days.

She stared out her window at the stark trees and wished she were back in Costa Rica in the sun. As she reached for her purse, her office door was flung open, bouncing off the wall. The force was so great she thought it would have slammed shut again except for the tall man standing in the doorway.

"Do you know who I am?" He reached her desk in two strides.

She looked up and nodded. "Senator Jake. Yes, we met in Austin when we took some students to observe the session." Adrienne kept her voice even, with little inflection. "Your son is one of my best students."

His face twisted, somewhere between a grimace and a laugh. He hadn't bothered to take off his black overcoat or remove his gloves. Leaning forward, he placed his fists on the edge of her desk. "Yes. My son. I want to know what lies you've been telling him. Just who do you think you are?"

Pulling her chair back to the desk, Adrienne looked at the rigid man who seemed to barely hold himself together. "Please, sir, if you want to discuss Bobby with me, I'd appreciate it if you'd sit down."

A large fist slammed into the wood of her desk, scattering papers. She grabbed her laptop before it shimmied to the floor.

"I am not here for a social visit or a student-parent review. You have filled my son with lies . . . lies that would kill his mother and ruin me. Lies that you are going to take back."

Adrienne stood up and moved away from the desk. She needed to get some distance from Jake while gaining some height. She still felt she could control the conversation. After all, she'd done nothing wrong. "Mr. Jake—"

"Senator." Jake's one word scorched the room.

"Senator Jake. I've not told Bobby any lies, especially none about you or your family. I don't know what you're talking about." She stared directly at him, willing him to control himself. Looking into his eyes that were almost slit shut, she wished she had her phone or a security button she could push.

He spoke through clenched jaws. "My boy accused me of having an affair with you. He said he had proof. Genetic proof."

She shivered as his guttural voice hit her. Was she really remembering that voice from twenty years ago? Could he have been there?

Still trying to pacify him, Adrienne raised her hand.

She gasped as he slapped it away and began moving around the desk. It took every ounce of control she had to keep her voice steady, to not give in to the crazy thoughts and the bile that was sitting at the back of her throat. "You have to calm down, Senator. Please, can we sit and talk?"

"I think there has been way too much talking already. What I need is for you to tell my son you were lying. I don't care what reason you give. I won't have you spreading rumors about us, about him, about me." He continued moving closer to her, until she finally broke and backed up toward the window.

It was only a few steps until her knees bumped against the display case under the window. She could retreat no further. Her Japanese dagger lay behind the glass. Would he really get violent? Did she need to protect herself?

Brushing against the side of the desk, Jake dislodged a pile of books, which hit the floor with a bang. Adrienne jumped as if shot. She was thrust back two decades to the basement in the UV fraternity house and the large man who walked in as she was being pinned down. He was the one who had hurt her. The one who still came in her nightmares and woke her with the taste of fear in her mouth.

"It was you. You were there. Bobby was right. Oh my God. You raped me. And then, what the hell? You tracked me down and adopted my baby?" Adrienne's fear had morphed into red anger. She pushed forward as if to strike Jake.

He grabbed her as she reached out. Pulling her around, he forced her arm up behind her back. "I don't know what you think you know, but it stops here."

She felt like her arm was going to break. Twisting around, she dragged an award off the windowsill and onto the display case. The shattering of the glass stopped Jake's rant. He released her arm. Breathing through the pain, she reached for the dagger.

Fumbling for the weapon, she cut her hand, and she dropped the dagger just as Bobby walked in, calling out, "Dr. Harrington, please, we need to talk." He pushed back the door and stopped.

The ten-by-ten office was overflowing with testosterone, and even at five foot ten, Adrienne was dwarfed by father and son.

"Dad! What the hell?" Bobby thrust into the room, circling the desk to get between his father and Adrienne. "Stop. Are you crazy? Dr. Harrington, you OK?"

Jake raised both hands as if to calm his son. "Bobby. Go home. We can speak there."

Bobby clenched his fists in response. "Hell, no. I'm not leaving until one of you tells me the truth. DNA doesn't lie. Mine says I'm related to both of you. How do you explain that?"

The senator stepped back, staring first at his son and then at Adrienne.

She moved further away from him, her hand reaching for a stone statue she'd recovered in Peru. "It's OK, Bobby. I think your father was just leaving. Right, Senator?"

The man nodded slowly.

Adrienne continued, one hand resting on the phone and the other holding the five-pound statue. "I promise we can talk tomorrow. Come back about 5:30. Go on home with your father."

"Dad?" Bobby moved closer to his father, his hand on his sleeve.

Senator Jake pulled Bobby into a one-armed hug and moved out of the office. Turning his head to glare once more at Adrienne, he got in the last word. "This isn't over, Professor. I'll protect my family, no matter what. I'm not without friends here. I can make this all go away."

"Is that a threat, Senator?"

"No, lady. It's a promise." At that, Senator Jake pushed his son through the door, slamming it as they left.

Letting out her breath for what felt like the first time in the last ten minutes, Adrienne sank back into her chair. Great, just what she needed, another enemy. Worse yet, an old enemy—literally her worst nightmare. For Bobby's accusation to be true, Senator Jake had to be the one . . . the shadow man haunting her dreams. The one who joined the drunken fraternity party and helped them rape a nineteen-year-old girl. Suddenly, her sweater and wool jacket offered no warmth.

Twenty-Two

HILDY
Present

GRACE WAS TWO MONTHS pregnant and already had a small baby bump. Embracing the current trend, she wore a horizontal-striped red and white sweater that pulled across her stomach. Pregnant or too much holiday celebration . . . maybe too early to differentiate, but her belly was on display, and I loved it!

I patted her shoulder as she made her third trip from the bathroom. The bathroom was one of the most frequented rooms during my pregnancy. Between nausea and peeing, I was in there every hour.

"I love your merry look." I grinned, placing a Santa hat on her head.

"Too late for this season." Grace whipped off the hat. "We're almost to Mardi Gras and purple and green. I knew I should have gotten this sweater in eggplant."

Was she was skipping over Valentine's Day because her romance novel didn't have an ending yet? I knew she still hadn't contacted Brad about the baby. Grace's enthusiasm for tracking down answers to Adrienne's death was probably a ploy to avoid dealing with her own reality. There was time, half a year. I'd keep working on her to reach out to the baby's father.

"Mom, come over here. I think I've found something." Grace pushed the computer chair back to the desk and hit the space bar, bringing the screen back to life on a news website. "This is from 2002. The *Cavalier Daily* is the independent student and community newspaper for Charlottesville and the University of Virginia. It gets no university funds, so the campus has little oversight or control over what they print."

Grace swung her chair back to me as she verified her source. "I decided to do a search on Adrienne at UVA around the time she dropped out. The paper covered the fraternity attack. No one was ever charged, but the fraternity was put on a six-month probation for alleged misconduct. The paper reported that the students at UVA were pissed at the relatively mild rebuke."

I leaned in, reading over her shoulder. "Definitely long before #MeToo was founded."

"Yeah, but look what I did find. A picture of the fraternity and some alumni at an earlier function. Look at the guy in the back row on the right. Does he remind you of anyone?" Grace pulled the screen around and increased the size of the newspaper photo by 100 percent, just before the pixels started breaking up.

"Oh my God!" I screamed then threw my hand over my mouth. Placing my hand on Grace's stomach, I mumbled, "Sorry, baby girl, I'm trying to clean up my language before you get here."

Grace snorted at me as I barreled on through.

"But OMG, is that Senator Jake, back in his mini-Afro days? He looks at least ten years older than those frat boys. He must be an alum. He—heck, we could probably blackmail him over his haircut alone."

Finally sitting down in the chair next to Grace, I stared at the screen and then spun around and looked at the whiteboard with the photos of Adrienne and Bobby.

I was about to really step in it. I wore my red power suit to the third memorial celebrating the life of Robert E. Jake Jr. The one I was not invited to attend. I'd helped pull together the campus memorial in the basketball arena the week after the deaths. That one felt the most sincere. I wore black for that one. His family had another service the following Sunday at the megachurch they attended. That one called for my dark gray pantsuit. The mostly Black congregation was awash in primary colors with great hats and head wraps. That one also felt pretty real.

This event, on the other hand was totally political. It ostensibly was to commemorate Bobby's twentieth birthday. The actual date was still weeks away, but there was a break in the legislative session, so the senator moved the event. It was in his home, the one that put the other River Oaks mansions to shame. I swear it could have housed a fraternity. And for this event, they'd added a full cadre of valet parkers, caterers, greeters, and excessive security.

I was crashing the party. If luck was with me, I'd find a lull in the festivities to corner the senator and ask about his UVA fraternity twenty years ago. The celebration might turn out to be connected to both Bobby's birth and his conception.

I found myself loaded down with wine and hors d'oeuvres. As many receptions as I'd attended over the past twenty-plus years, it was still almost impossible to balance a glass of wine and a small plate while conducting any kind of business. Taking a sip of the wine, I set it on the high-top along with the plate. Senator Jake was across the room. How many people would stop me on the way over to him? Before I could set out, a hand gripped my shoulder.

The security guy was well over six foot and easily 280 pounds. "Can I see your invitation, Miss?" His voice graveled like it was filtered through tobacco and whiskey.

"Oh, invitation? I didn't realize this was a closed event. I'd seen it on the news and thought I'd have an opportunity to offer my condolences to the Jakes." I gave the gorilla my friendliest, most innocent smile.

"You'll have to come with me, Miss. You need to leave. You can go out that door there. It will lead around the house to the front where the valet can bring up your car." He waved at an evidently lesser security person. "Ms. Stuart will escort you out to make sure you don't get lost."

Nothing I could do but nod and follow behind the woman to the front of the house. I hadn't used the valet, so she left me at the curb. I headed down the street to where I'd found a parking place, two blocks over. *I shouldn't have worn these damn high-heeled boots. I'll be lucky if I don't break my ankle.* I kept my eyes down as I walked to avoid any potholes or other ankle-breaking possibilities.

I breathed a sigh of relief at making it to my car in one piece. A hand grabbed my shoulder as I reached for the door handle. The fingers pushed into my flesh like talons, and I stopped dead. I could see his wrist and the pin-striped suit over a monogrammed sleeve—POD. The hand was large, hairy but not calloused, manicured nails. Strong enough to bring me to a full stop. I pushed against the arm and squirmed enough to see my captor. I wasn't that surprised to see the senator's aide behind me.

Dirk . . . no . . . Patrik, I thought. Yes, POD for Patrik O. Daniel.

"I don't like being touched," I said.

"That's the least of your problems." His fingers dug more firmly into my shoulder. "Senator Jake and his family just lost their son. They don't need you poking your nose in. We will stop you, one way or another."

I turned enough to bring my heel down hard onto the top of his dress loafer. His face changed to surprise bordering on pain. His grip slipped, but he still held tight to my elbow. Instead of pulling away, I moved closer to him, swinging my fisted left hand into his groin. That did it. His arm dropped protectively to his crotch, and I was free. I was amazed that move really worked.

Thanks, Chief West, for the personal defense course.

I pulled open the door and threw myself behind the wheel, hitting the lock as I jerked it shut. Daniel glared through the window, finally turning back to the senator's house. Then the shaking began. I stared at my hands clenching the steering wheel. A lingering smell of cherry tobacco wafted up from my sleeve. I remembered that smell.

I was in Adrienne's garage . . . groggy from the attack. I remembered pushing myself from the floor, smelling stale gasoline, musty laundry, and something more. Rather than worrying about some weird smell that didn't belong, I needed my vision to focus. After staring at the dirty concrete floor, I had leaned against the dryer and limped to the side door. I smelled it then, the sweetness of the tobacco, so out of place.

He'd been there. I was sure of it. What was a state senator's aide doing in the garage of my dead friend? *Obvious,* I thought. *He was searching for something.* Had he grabbed me then as well?

I shook my head and brought my olfactory search back to the here and now. I left the party with my dignity barely intact. Still no answers. Did Senator Jake really know Adrienne when she was an undergraduate? The old newspaper article showed he was connected to UVA at the time . . . and to the fraternity where Adrienne was raped.

Once in my house, I immediately pulled off my boots. Great for weapons, hell for walking.

Shasta did her usual bouncing until I reached down. She smelled my hand for any possible treats and gave me a lick to replenish her scent in case some other dog had rubbed against me.

My mind was still flipping through wild scenarios. Rape. Adoptions. DNA. Revenge.

In the kitchen I pulled a bottle of French rosé from my wine fridge. I had missed out on the food at the memorial party, so I scooped up a bag of pita chips, some hummus, grapes, and a small wheel of brie. Perfect late-night munch and brain food for working the imagination. Piling my goodies on a plate, I grabbed a wine glass and a cheese knife, and my picnic was ready to lay out on the coffee table.

Shasta watched closely as I set down my food at a level she could reach. She had a special love of cheese, though too much gave her gas. Pushing her nose away, I dropped onto the couch.

I pulled my legs up and snuggled back into the corner. Shasta immediately found her own cuddle space between my knees and the back of the sofa. She dropped her head on my knee and stared intently at the myriad pleasures only a few feet away. I broke a chip in half and shared it with her.

My first swallow of wine brought a flash of Provence to mind, before Shasta's cold nose reminded me that she also loved green grapes. "OK, but just one. And no cheese, too close to bedtime." Like she'd pay any attention to that.

Seeing my red boots by the door jolted me back to the evening's main event. I could only imagine the repercussions to Senator Jake's run for the governor's mansion. He was easily the front-runner for the Republican ticket. It would totally derail any political plans if it was proved he'd fathered a child due to the gang rape of a college coed. No matter that it occurred twenty years ago.

Such a scoop would have certainly catapulted Tremayne's career into the national spotlight. It also would be worth some serious bucks if used for blackmail. Either way, the senator would pay mightily. The pieces were almost fitting. Not hard to imagine Tremayne blackmailing the senator over Bobby's parentage. And I could maybe believe Jake would lash out and remove his blackmailer. But would he actually get his hands bloody? Could he have killed his son? Even accidently?

My head was beginning to go into overload, and the wine wasn't really helping. I needed sleep even more than I needed munchies, so, with one last treat for Shasta, I put the cheese and fruit back in the fridge and left the rest on the counter to clean up tomorrow.

I barely remembered brushing my teeth or pulling off my bra before I was face-planted in the middle of my bed with Shasta curved into the small of my back. Down for the count.

Twenty-Three

SUNLIGHT STREAMED THROUGH THE window, hitting me right in the face. It hurt to open my eyes, so I rolled over and pretended it was not way past my usual alarm. I must have punched the snooze button four times . . . a personal best.

Shasta was bouncing on the rug near my head, emitting a small whine aimed at making me feel guilty to have slept past her outdoor break time. She was generally willing to wait when I wasn't home, but mornings were all about her bathroom run and breakfast.

I pushed myself up and swung my legs over the bed. I needed caffeine badly if I was going to make it through the day. Feet in slippers, half-clothed body in robe, I shuffled toward the kitchen and the back door. No walk today, just a run in the yard and peeing in the back bushes. "We'll do four blocks after work to make up for it," I promised the dog.

Coffee started, I moved to the front porch to retrieve the newspaper. The first of four I read daily. The *Houston Chronicle* had the usual page one crime reports and fatal shootings. It also previewed the social section with a headline touting the story on the Jakes' birthday-memorial soiree. I grabbed my coffee as the pod machine gurgled to a stop, doctored it with a glug of creamer, and savored my first swallow. My eyes were now fully open and ready to review the reporter's version of the senator's event. The day was still somewhat mellow, so I moved to my deck to get caffeinated and informed.

Focusing on the list of VIP attendees, I noted the Gulf U president and some of his VPs, plus the usual political hangers-on and wannabes. I'd seen most of them the previous night. Staring more closely at the photos, I realized that Mrs. Jake was not in a single picture. Come to think of it, I couldn't remember seeing her when I made my way through their home. Shouldn't she have been at Senator Jake's side?

Checking my watch, I decided it wasn't too early to call an expert.

"Morning, Mother. I hope I didn't wake you." I don't know why every time I talked to her, my back and shoulders got rigid—very straight but rigid.

"Of course not, Hildegard. I'm always up by 6:30 to do my yoga. And Cam next door comes at 7:00 to pick up Minuit for their morning run. Shouldn't you be at work by now?"

I swear she has radar vision and can see from her kitchen to my back deck.

"That's Cameron Mitchell, right?" *Maybe I can distract her with this.* Though I didn't really believe it. "He's chairman of Gulf U's Board of Regents. I didn't know he was also a dog walker. Though it might be a bit awkward to have my board chair walk Shasta. Anyway, I'm taking off today. And why couldn't I have been calling you from my office?"

"Birds, my girl. I can hear the birds. So what brings you to me on your day off?" She was using her patient-adult-to-child voice, which always managed to get under my skin. You'd think, after fifty years, she'd stop talking down to me. You'd think, after fifty years, I'd stop caring about that.

"I want to run a few things by you, if you have time. Something doesn't feel right, but I might be missing the upper-echelon nuances of it all." Not sure I could be more oblique.

"Fine. Always pleased to help. Stop by Baked Off and pick up some cinnamon rolls on your way."

Before I could do more than nod, the connection dropped. I'd received my orders. Saluting the phone, I stopped long enough to rub Shasta's head and invite her into the backyard. Oops, back to my room to put on a bra and some somewhat Mother-worthy clothes.

One stop later, I pulled into the drive off Heights Boulevard. I pulled my purse over my shoulder and grabbed the pink pastry box as I scooted out of my car. It was a bit worse for wear, but it was all mine. It did look sad next to Mother's land yacht town car. Grace was in the window of her garage apartment, and I waved for her to join us.

The brainpower of three Brentwood women was a force that could conquer any problem. At least that's what I hoped. I had to be close to finding the answer, the one that did not have Adrienne killing Bobby and herself. It should have been obvious to even the thickest-headed police, particularly after Tremayne's murder. But no. West said he had plenty of enemies, and they saw no reason to connect the dots.

"They are about to close the case, and my friend will officially be branded a murderer." My jaw clenched. Did I say that out loud? I marched through the back gate to the kitchen door.

"Hildegard, there is no need to shout. You sound like a heathen, and I can hear perfectly well." Mother looked over the top of her reading glasses with a quelling gaze. She'd have made the best librarian ever. She had the whisper power and the lifelong book affair going for her.

Grace trailed in after me, grinning. She loved watching Mother and me do our thing.

I waved her in behind me and closed the door. With the rolls on the marble counter, I moved to the stove and pulled the copper tea kettle onto a burner. Grace went to the cupboard and brought out three dessert plates and mugs with their different botanical designs. I loved my mother's Portmeirion pottery. It felt like spring.

We'd practiced this routine often. Mother sailed into the kitchen just as the tea kettle whistled. I poured the hot water into the Portmeirion teapot, and Grace added the tea caddy with the Earl Grey. The cream went into the pitcher, and the sugar and sugar substitute were already on the counter. We were all set up at the island and took our assigned seats . . . Mother, Grace, and then me.

No one said a thing between that initial salvo and taking a first sip of the fragrant tea. A collective sigh later, we each sat back on our bar stools and smiled the same satisfied grin. Home and family. Nothing else mattered.

I sighed again. *Why don't we do this more often?* With another sip of the scalding tea, I pulled my thoughts back to the issue at hand. Pinching a bit of cinnamon roll, I pulled Grace in for a hug, which she quickly deflected.

"OK, Mom, you've got our attention. Why the confab?" Grace was always the one to cut to the chase with little or no sugarcoating.

"Yes, Hildegarde. You said you needed a consult. I can't imagine you need help with some upcoming PR event, so it must have something to do with this infernal investigation you've pulled us into." Now Mother was using her CEO no-nonsense voice.

I gave one more deep sigh before getting down to business. "So, OK, guilty as charged. I refuse to stand by and see Adrienne's name shredded. It is all circumstantial. She is as much a victim here as Bobby Jake."

I took another hit of Earl Grey and continued. "I need to find the link between their murders and Jack Tremayne's death. At least no one can accuse Adrienne of that murder. If I can show the connection, I'll negate all the assumptions the police have accepted regarding her involvement with Bobby."

I looked at my mother and daughter, hoping to see some support. Perhaps a glimmer in Grace's reporter's eye.

"Well, we can go over the murder board in my apartment again to see if something makes better sense." Even if she was just pacifying me, I was glad for her support.

Then Mother erupted. "Hildegard Brentwood. You are risking your job over this. Didn't the president specifically order you to stand down? How is he going to react when he finds you've disobeyed his directive?" She took a moment for another sip of tea and a dainty bite of roll.

Grace's eyes jumped between us like she was watching a tennis match.

I launched my final salvo. "Where do you think I got my stubborn streak—my need to find truth, no matter what? I remember stories of a young firebrand standing off police at an anti-war rally at UT in 1968. Isn't that where you met Father?" *That should get her juices flowing!*

Grace swung her head back. "Woe, Grand. I never heard that story. I thought you were always your put-together self, very Junior

League. Did you really freak out during the Vietnam protests? Are there any pictures?" Her grin practically split her face.

"It was the right thing to do. And yes, I was suspended for a week and missed my history final. But we were right to protest, even if I had to retake that damn course." Now it was Mother who looked both self-righteous and a bit sheepish.

My grin now matched Grace's. "Gotcha! Some things are worth risking your comfort for, and I believe in my heart that this is as critical as your war protests." I reached across Grace and touched Mother's hand. "You helped make people aware of what was happening ten thousand miles from Austin, Texas. On a more personal level, I want to make people understand what really happened that afternoon in Adrienne's office. It's worth risking administrative wrath."

Grace added her hand to mine and Mother's. We were all in.

"Now, back to this murder board." Mother glared at both of us. "I suppose we should go up there to finish this discussion."

Mother swept past us and headed to the outside stairs leading to Grace's newly adopted apartment. We followed like ducklings.

Grace's apartment was finally set up, her furniture, art, and memorabilia all in their assigned spots. It was one large room over the three-car garage. Her gourmet kitchen looked out on the lush garden in the back of Mother's Victorian. It was all Grace, with her red leather couch and teal chairs facing a wall of bookcases, a sixty-inch screen in the middle. The shelves were filled with her collection of illustrated children's books, which she'd been collecting since she was two—I started her early. Her journalism awards, family photos—including a new one of her first ultrasound—and sculpture and art pieces from all over the world. What few walls she had were covered in paintings from Texas artists. Antique rugs warmed up the room.

Mother marched across the floor to the back corner where Grace had her remote office. In addition to the usual computer and monitors, she had a ring light with a small camera in the center to handle her blog and other online videos. At that moment, the white board faced the wall.

Grace rolled it to the center of the room. We pulled up chairs from the dining table and stared at the photos linked together by markers to notes and each other. I stood and used a small magnet to attach the article I'd clipped about the Jakes' latest gathering.

"Hildegard, remind me what you brought us here to do."

Don't let her get to you, I repeated a few times to myself. *Breathe deeply and carry on.* A quick shake of my shoulders, and I moved past her tone. "Well, Mother. I *dragged* you up here to help me understand how Mrs. Jake didn't make it to her only son's memorial birthday celebration last night." I stood back to wait for the inevitable pushback.

As expected, Mother shook her head, no doubt sure I was mistaken.

I continued before she could interrupt. "Really, look at the photos in the *Chronicle.* She's not in any of them. I admit I was only there a few minutes before Jake's bully boys ushered me off the premises. I saw you across the ballroom. I got ejected before I could speak to you, which was probably a good thing. It keeps you free from my *persona non grata* status. I'm sure you stayed through the speeches anyway. Did you see the senator's wife at any time?"

Before she could respond, I dropped my next bit of proof. "I spent this morning searching through a gazillion photos posted by attendees and their staffs to prove they were all there paying their respects. Mrs. Jake does not appear in any of them."

Grace pulled out her phone and began her own search.

I turned to my daughter. "Gracie, I think you'll find that there has been no public sighting of Cecily Jake since the second church-based memorial service, and that was over a week ago."

I stood back for my aha moment as Mother went to pull the article from the board. The society editor hadn't speculated about Cecily's absence, but she had recorded all the prominent players in the room, and Mrs. Jake was not mentioned.

Putting Cecily's photo on the board, I wrote a large question mark under it. Turning back to my audience, I waved the red marker. "I can't imagine she had anything to do with Bobby's death, but would she have gone after Adrienne to shut her up about Bobby's parentage and he was in the wrong place at the wrong time?"

Mother looked up from the article. "I'm not that close to Cecily. We've played tennis and served on some of the same boards. She's always been wound pretty tight. I suppose she could have gone off the deep end. Who wouldn't when losing her son?" She tapped her fuchsia nail on the article a few times. "Frankly, I could see Robert going berserk before Cecily. He has much more to lose politically if it got out that the Right's chosen man of color had a bastard child. And if that child was the result of rape, he might never recover."

Grace looked ready to jump in, but Mother took a quick breath and waved her hand. "Let me call around to some friends and the salon. Someone has to have seen her. I'll try to get into the *castle* again and offer my sympathies to both of them. I'll report back as soon as I have information." She was now standing and heading for the door.

Mother was perfect for this assignment, and in the meantime, Grace and I could continue our internet search of the senator's background and his current location. And I wanted to officially add Patrik Daniel to the board.

"Who's that?" Grace looked up from her keyboard to focus on Daniel's face. I'd copied it from one of the event photos in the *Chronicle*, so it was a bit fuzzy.

"Patrik Daniel," I pronounced as I wrote his name under the photo. "Jake's chief aide. He accosted me at my car last night. Veiled threats. That fist to the groin move we learned in our Safe Woman class works." I grinned at the memory of Daniel hunched over, eyes crossed.

Grace started to stand. "Mom! Are you OK? Did he hurt you? We need to call the cops."

Shaking my head, I kept us on task. "I'm fine. He was the one who limped home. A spiked bootheel to the instep and fist to the groin got me loose and into my car with the locks engaged." As I spoke, I drew a line from Daniel's photo to the shot of Adrienne's trashed living room.

Grace followed my marker with a quizzical stare, raising her hand like a student. "OK, now I'm really lost. How did you get from his bully attack on you to the destruction of Adrienne's home?"

"Cherry tobacco. He grabbed my arm and shoulder, and I ended up close to his jacket. He smelled like pipe tobacco, the sweet, cherry kind." I stopped at my deductive moment, and she stared at me. "Oh, sorry. You can't see into my head. I noticed it last night, as he was manhandling me. I got another whiff of it once I got home. I was drinking wine and trying to find a way past my job, Shasta as usual was sucking up for cheese. She stopped and licked my arm where Daniels had grabbed me. I could still smell his pipe tobacco."

I could tell Grace was getting annoyed with my stringing this out. Speeding up, I continued. "The smell triggered a quick flashback to when I woke up in Adrienne's garage after the attack and trashing of her house. It was the weird smell I couldn't translate, but it came back in a rush last night—cherry-infused pipe tobacco. I'm sure Patrik Daniel was there. He had to be responsible for the crude search of Adrienne's house. Probably looking for her files from Ancestors.com."

Grace stood and walked over to the board, putting her nose right up against Daniel's photo. "We need to know more about him." Turning back to her desk, she hunched over, her fingers flying over the keyboard.

"Patrik Oliver Daniel." She began reading from the state senate website. "He's been with Jake for his entire career, started right out of college. Graduate of UVA, same fraternity but ten years later."

I drew another line from Daniel to the group frat photo, searching through the thumbnail face shots to tentatively circle a husky kid in the back row.

"Could he have been part of the gang rape?" I stared at the picture as if expecting an answer. "It would explain a lot. He would know the history. He would want to preserve the myth as much as the senator."

Grace nodded, her fingers continuing to speed across the keyboard. "Yeah, here's his UVA file." She paused a second, scanning the screen. "Says here he dropped out a semester into his junior year. When he came back the next fall, he buckled down with twenty hours and graduated with his class. Looks like he received a full-ride scholarship for his senior year. Anonymous donor."

Now I drew a circle around his face on the photo with a line to Jake. "He had to know. I'd lay money on him being a part of the gang rape. Bet Jake was the anonymous donor. Kept it all in the family, so to speak."

Her face scrunched up in concentration, Grace cocked an eyebrow at me. "Innocent until proven guilty. Remember?"

"Of course." I shook my head trying to clear out the picture of the frat house basement. "It's just speculation at this point, but damn good speculation. I know he has the temper trigger to set him off. My upper arm still has his fingerprints all over it." I rubbed the wounded appendage as I continued. "In truth, he has as much to lose as Jake—he's his ticket to the statehouse and maybe Washington."

Pulling my fingers through my hair, I paced in front of the board. "You know, Daniel could get around everywhere with little fanfare or recognition. Who notices the political aides? Could he do this without Jake knowing?" I was now mumbling more to myself than to Grace.

"I've thought all along that Bobby's death was an accident. He walked into the attack on Adrienne and got in the way. What if they were both targeted? In some ways, it makes more sense. Either person could have been killed more easily somewhere else. But to catch them together and be able to stage the murder-suicide scene made her office the ideal locale. That would make it premeditated, and I do have a problem thinking Robert Jake would purposely kill his only son and heir."

I was back in front of Daniel's picture on the board. Tapping my marker on his nose, I turned to Grace. She stared at me as if I'd gone loco.

"How does your mind work, Mom? That is the most convoluted motive I've heard yet. Kinda amazing but positively Machiavellian. And hell to prove."

Pushing back from the desk, she walked into her small but well-appointed kitchen. "Break time. Want tea or something cold?" Grace opened the fridge stocked with water, soft drinks, and beer. Her wine storage was on the other side of her gourmet Viking gas stove. I was sorry it was too early for wine.

"Just a fizzy water for me. Lime if you have it." She pulled out the flavored seltzer for me and a diet ginger ale for herself. "Definitely time to pull out our secret weapon," she said.

I had to grin at Grace's newest title for her grandmother. "She's already tracking Cecily. Let's flag her to keep her eye out for Daniel. Interesting to get Cecily's take on him." My thumbs were clicking away on my iPhone as I sent an update text to my mother. *It will be interesting to see what the gossip queen of Houston can discover in her wanderings through the halls of the rich and wannabe famous,* I thought.

I settled back on the couch to hydrate and contemplate. We'd eliminated a number of my original suspects. Drawing an X across each photo as we verified alibis, I ticked them off one by one.

- Jack Tremayne was now a victim. We'd moved him to the other side of the board.
- Adrienne's ex, Darrell Kinkaid, supposedly was drunk and raging at a campus watering hole, but back in Virginia. I'd heard from a number of people who had heard him

cursing Adrienne and his life. His photo remained in its place while we verified his location, but it looked like he was off the hook.

- × Smarmy Gustav Minor seemed to be in the clear. The department records showed him presenting a paper at a conference in Seattle when the murders occurred. He'd been the first to get marked off, much to my regret. I'd have loved to see him go down.
- ✓ The Jakes, both Robert and Cecily, and now Patrik Daniel remained suspects.

My gut told me it was one or all of them in some weird political conspiracy. Something needed to break soon. My radar was pinging. The administration was going to figure out I was still working on the investigation. I was already under orders to desist detecting and get this off the front page of the newspapers. One last blast of headlines, I hoped, would exonerate Adrienne and name the real murderer.

OK, Mother. You wanted in on this. Seems like you're the key to us getting the proof we need. I'm up against a brick wall of obfuscation and red tape, not to mention general hostility. Adrienne and I are counting on you.

I sent my silent prayer into the ether as I sat waiting to see what Victoria could do when set loose.

Twenty-Four

VICTORIA

Present

"MRS. BRENTWOOD. WELCOME BACK. It's been too long since we've seen you at the club." The white-coated doorman gushed as he held open the door.

Victoria Brentwood moved effortlessly among the rich and famous. Daughter of one of the founding families of the Heights, she'd married well. On her husband's death, she successfully took over his oilfield services company, growing it into one of the top firms in the Southwest. She'd retired three years before, only to get back in the fray as chair of the board of Houston's major charitable foundation.

Nothing she loved more than to tweak the mighty and pretentious. The Houston Country Club had plenty of both. Nodding to the liveried doorman, she smiled. "Miles. Good to see you. I stopped in for a quick lunch. Have you seen Mrs. Jake today? I called her home, and her housekeeper said she had a meeting here. I was hoping to offer my condolences . . . and see if there is anything she needs."

He moved closer and lowered his voice. "Indeed. What a tragedy. I can't imagine how she is holding up. But she's putting on a brave face. I think she came in this morning for a meeting about the upcoming Children's Charity Gala. Good to get her mind off. You might catch her in the Tejas Room. I think that's where they were meeting."

Victoria barely noticed the wall hangings or the large paintings depicting riding to the hunt. The Houston Country Club leaned heavily to the old-money set . . . oil barons and land developers. She'd been a part of all that initially through her husband's oil field services business and after his death on her own terms. She didn't need directions to the Tejas Room, striding quietly across the old Persian rug to the thick runner that covered the main hallway.

Not surprisingly, the doorman had called it. As she approached the room, it was in the process of giving up a number of well-coifed and -outfitted ladies who lunch. This was truly the power that ran Houston. Even in the cowboy past, the women ran the ranches, everything outside the actual roundups. They were still a scary, secret force in Houston. One never worth underestimating.

Victoria stood to the side as three women exited, turning back to persuade another to join them for lunch. One of them saw her and waved a brief hello as they marched in step to the tearoom.

Cecily was still seated, alone in the now emptied room. She looked confused, seemingly not sure where she was or what she was doing there. Victoria moved slowly toward her, as if approaching a wild or injured animal. Injured to be sure. She couldn't imagine how she would recover from the loss of her daughter or granddaughter. And Cecily's son had been murdered.

Her approach didn't seem to register on Cecily Jake. Victoria sat at the table and gently touched her arm, causing Cecily to jerk back in her chair. Her eyes took a moment to focus and recognize the person invading her space. As she settled again, Victoria patted her arm and leaned closer.

"I have no words that could possibly make a difference in the pain you are experiencing. That's probably as it should be, because no one should have to go through this kind of horror. There shouldn't be easy words to explain it or make it better." Victoria spoke slowly, quietly.

Cecily seemed to appreciate the truth in those words, looking into Victoria's eyes, her own brimming with tears. She laid her head on her arms and sighed with a heaviness that carried all the world's sorrow.

"I really don't know why I came here today," Cecily said, talking more to herself than to Victoria. "I was worse than useless to the charity committee. I made them all fidget, not wanting to address the elephant in the room and not sure how to avoid it. I just needed some relief, something else to capture my mind."

She sat back up and stared down at her hands, rubbing her wedding band. "Robert has been so worried and focused on ensuring that Bobby is properly remembered. I woke this morning for the first time without the haze of the drugs the doctor prescribed. I think for the first time, I realized he was truly gone from me. He was my light, my life, my all. Now what? I guess I hoped I could focus on this event . . . the good the money will do. But I was worthless . . . less than worthless . . . I stopped all discussions."

Cecily twisted her hands and returned to rubbing her wedding ring. It was the symbol of her worth, her marriage, her husband, and her family, which was now reduced to just the two of them.

Victoria nodded, not wanting to stop the woman's personal assessment.

"I hate all the sympathy, all the black arm bands, grave expressions. I can see behind them, the relief that this was my tragedy . . . one they had blessedly escaped."

Victoria heard the rattle of dishes being wheeled from the banquet room down the hall. A glance at her watch told her the tearoom was closing soon. Ah, well, she could grab something later. Her attention returned to Cecily, who was trying to stand and gather her things. If she was going to get any information to help Hildy, she needed to keep Cecily talking.

"How is Robert doing? You have to be holding it all together for him as well as for yourself."

Dropping back into her chair, Cecily's brow wrinkled. "Robert. Robert has the legislative session to distract him. He's back in Austin right now for a vote on something or other he helped sponsor. I never bother keeping up with his political doings. Patrik is good at letting me know when I need to do anything with other wives or at an event or something."

She no longer seemed to be speaking to Victoria. Her eyes were slightly glazed, out of focus. "My role is hearth and home. I built my life around Bobby. I knew he'd be heading out on his own in a few years, but then I could hope for grandchildren to spoil. I wasn't prepared for it ending so abruptly, so finally."

"You can't punish yourself for not anticipating something so harrowing. No one could," Victoria said reaching over to touch her gently again. "Tell me about Bobby. What was he like as a child?"

"We had tried so hard to have a baby. Robert desperately wanted a son to carry on the Jake name and tradition. I thought when we learned I couldn't conceive, he might leave me, find someone else."

Victoria sat up straighter. This was the first she'd heard about Bobby not being Cecily's biological son. Hildy suspected something, but Cecily now confirmed it. Could this be a reason for his death?

The grieving woman continued speaking, more to herself than to Victoria. "Then Bobby happened. Robert just showed up one day with this tiny miracle in his arms. Patrik Daniel's father was a close friend. He was the one who explained that Robert had learned one of his cousins was pregnant and considering an abortion. He intervened, helped her with money to get good prenatal care and start her on a path to find work. Bobby was two days old when he was placed in my arms. My heart opened, and he filled the huge hole in it. He was mine. He was all mine."

Prompting her to continue, Victoria asked, "Did he grow up knowing he was adopted?"

Cecily looked up as if just remembering she was not alone. "No. No, we were his parents . . . his mother and father. He even looked like Robert . . . same nose and mouth. The Jake genes are hardy. Bobby was always ours, only ours. And Robert began grooming him for greatness as soon as he could walk and talk. He was the golden child . . . the one to carry the Jake name to new heights. Gone. All gone." Cecily choked out the last phrase.

Victoria went over to the conference table where the charity meeting had happened. She picked up the carafe of water, poured a glass, and handed it to Cecily.

"Thanks," she said, holding the glass with both hands. Taking a sip, she carefully placed it back on the table. "I don't understand any of this. And why was Bobby with his teacher? Classes weren't in session. He should have been with his friends. None of this makes any sense."

Cecily shook her head as if clearing out the cobwebs. Straightening her spine, she stood and again gathered her purse and notebook. "I'm sorry, I really have to go now. I need to go home . . . to see what I'm supposed to do now."

Victoria helped her down the hall to the reception area. "Miles, can you get someone to bring up Mrs. Jake's car? Thanks." She nodded at him while keeping an arm around Cecily, who looked even more fragile than she had earlier.

"Aren't these beautiful?" Cecily touched the soft pink camellia in the huge floral arrangement on the round antique table. "These don't grow well in Houston, you know. But they are still my favorite."

Miles returned and helped Cecily down the marble steps and into her car. He'd had the valet bring Victoria's town car to the circular drive as well. She handed him ten dollars as she settled into the leather seat. "Thanks, Miles. Would you mind calling Senator Jake's home and letting them know she has left the country club? They can keep an eye out for her."

As he nodded agreement, Victoria put her car in gear. She headed out of River Oaks, up Allen Parkway along the bayou leading to the glass and steel metropolis—downtown Houston. She loved to turn on Waugh, where tourists stopped every night to watch a quarter million Mexican bats fly from under the bridge in search of insects. Too early to join the bat watchers, not that she ever planned to do that. Victoria followed Waugh over the bayou where it became Heights Boulevard . . . her path home.

“Call Hildegard.” Victoria spoke to her car. Voice mail. She really hated when all this high-tech stuff didn’t instantly get her what she wanted. Waiting for the beep, she told her daughter to gather Grace and meet in the *auxiliary war room* she’d set up in her garden atrium.

It was heading toward spring, which in Houston started immediately after the rodeo and Galveston’s Mardi Gras. Victoria had set up a copy of the whiteboard Hildy and Grace had created in Grace’s apartment. It was a grisly contrast to the green ferns and budding azaleas in her backyard, but she needed the evidence of the coming warmth to counteract the chilling reality posted on the board.

She’d wait for her daughter to update the board with this new information. Victoria settled in the comfortable wicker rocker, looking out onto her lush garden. Even in the throes of winter, there was always something to catch her eye. A group of robins perched on the lip of one of the fountains. *Flying back north after their respite here in warmer climes,* she thought as they splashed and rolled in the water. Grasping for something uplifting to engage her mind, she noted the difference in fountain etiquette each bird species exhibited. Robins were splashers; mourning doves were sippers, carefully dipping their beaks into the water; and blue jays were the bullies of the garden, puffing up and pushing the others away from the water.

She supposed she could assign similar traits to the suspects Hildy and Grace had identified. Cecily was definitely the dove in mourning . . . just sipping at life. Senator Jake was a closet robin . . . holding himself tight to avoid getting rowdy. She wondered if Patrik were the blue jay. He’d certainly played the bully, threatening Hildy at the memorial service.

Twenty-Five

HILDY

Present

"OK, MOTHER. WE'RE HERE. Have you got something for us? How was Mrs. Jake?" I swallowed hard, my voice squeaking as I rushed into the glass room.

Victoria looked up and smiled at her daughter. She was about to rise when Grace glided into the room. "Sit, Grand. Stay comfortable. Let me get us some tea and maybe a cookie or two. Mom, chill a moment. I'll be right back, and you can't start without me."

I looked out the window, not really seeing the birds or fountains. Worrying. How much longer could I push this without jeopardizing my job?

Grace walked slowly back into the room with a large tray carrying a china pot, three mugs, and a plate of thin lemon cookies—homemade from the French bakery.

"Mom, come sit. I made chamomile. It should help calm you. I can feel your anxiety a block away."

I turned and smiled at my daughter. "When did you become the grown-up here?"

"Someone has to be, and since I'm working on becoming the best mother ever . . ." Grace looked down and gently smoothed the sweater over her growing baby bump.

A smile took over my face as I looked at my developing grandchild. A sudden thought intruded. *I need to pick the best name for myself before the baby comes. Mother is "Grand" and could morph into "Great-Grand." So perhaps "Nan" would work, as long as it didn't become "Nanny."*

It was enough to bring me back to the business at hand, so I took a seat around the wrought iron table in the middle of the room. "I'll pour, and Mother, you can report. I can't believe Mrs. Jake was back to business as usual—charity committees, galas."

"Oh, Hildegard, have some compassion for the poor woman. She looked gutted. Said she was there because she had to get away from the dead of the house, the pounding memories."

Mother picked up her mug like it was fine bone china, sipping slowly to keep from burning her tongue.

I tapped my foot, waiting for her to continue.

"I'm not sure why, but she seemed to need to unburden herself. In fact, it felt like she was talking more to herself than to me. The big news was she verified that Bobby was adopted and never knew it. Robert just showed up with a newborn baby one day. Patrik Daniel's father was the one who detailed how they came to do that . . . a pregnant young cousin . . . Robert paid her bills . . . an answer to their prayer. Private adoption. I don't think Cecily ever signed anything. No doubt Robert handled it all." Another quick swig of tea.

My hands cupped around the mug, pulling warmth into them. I'd walked-jogged the five blocks to Mother's house. It seemed faster at the time, but I was shivering now that the adrenaline had worn off. Lifting my hands, I took a gulp of the tea, welcoming the warmth as it slid down my throat.

"It seems to be coming together. Some of the students in my podcasting class have been talking to Bobby's friends. Bobby and his father didn't get along, according to his closest buds. The senator liked to show Bobby off to his friends and colleagues, like a trick pony. He literally paraded him through the statehouse every two years as the session got underway."

Shaking my head, imagining how Grace would react to such an invasion, I continued. "Cheryl Ann, my best senior, is loving this investigative role. She reported on the rumors going around that Bobby planned to make a scene this year at his presentation. It was all tied to his twentieth birthday, and he was planning on supplying primo drugs for party favors."

Mother set her mug down, gazing again into her garden. "That couldn't have gone down very well if Senator Jake found it out."

"Yeah. And it didn't sound like Bobby was trying to keep his plan any big secret—too many people were involved. With Jake positioning to run for governor, the last thing he'd want is his shiny bright son pissing all over the place, embarrassing him in front of the power brokers."

I stood, walking to the whiteboard, and filled in the dotted line between Adrienne and Bobby. I drew a new red line linking Jake with Daniel and then to Bobby. I also added a line in green between Cicely and Daniel. He seemed to be her primary information source.

"Wonder if there is anything going on between Daniel and Cicely?" I started to chew the end of the marker when Grace pulled it out of my hand.

"Saving you from permanent green lips, Mom." Grace grinned as she picked up the black marker and added some question marks under Patrik Daniel's name.

"Do we know how far back Daniel and Jake go?" she asked, looking between her grandmother and me.

Mother piped up. "Didn't his bio indicate he began working for Jake's campaign office just out of college. UVA, like Jake and like Adrienne. Same fraternity. Jake was an alum advisor when Daniel was a student. Cecily mentioned he was involved in the adoption. I think Daniel's father and Jake were from the same neighborhood in Virginia. If so, they probably knew each other Daniel's entire life."

Victoria took the marker from Grace. She wrote University of Virginia on the board and drew lines from Jake and Daniel to the school. She then added a line from Adrienne to UVA, linking the three of them.

I took over the tale and let Mother play recording secretary. "Adrienne's aunt admitted she'd been raped at a UVA frat party. She also told me that the rape resulted in a pregnancy. Her family insisted she relinquish the child and quickly set up a private adoption. It was another year before she transferred to Virginia Tech to complete her degree."

Could it be that bizarre? Could those actions and people in Virginia all converge in Houston two decades later? If Bobby was really Adrienne's son, who besides Robert Jake and Patrik Daniel would know it? Looking at the board, it was clear there were fewer than the standard six degrees of separation between all these characters.

All we had was conjecture, circumstantial evidence at best. I got up and moved my mother aside. Standing at the board in my best professorial manner, I hit the marker on each name. "This feels like the most significant motive we've found."

Marching back and forth in front of the board, I continued my lecture. "Looking at our list of suspects, we've eliminated most of them. We know Adrienne's ex was back in Virginia trying to dig out of his plagiarism troubles. Dr. Minor is a certifiable misogynist, but he couldn't get energized enough to throw a punch, let alone murder a very fit woman and strong student. And he was in Seattle, presenting a paper. He was definitely clear. And of course that lying, blackmailing, media scum Jack Tremayne was proved innocent when he got himself murdered."

Grace broke into my diatribe. "Wait. Don't the police believe Tremayne's killing was not connected to the campus one?"

Shaking my head, I circled Tremayne's name and crossed it off. "Of course, they have to believe that if they still hold with the murder-suicide of Adrienne and Bobby. And that just makes no sense. Why would Adrienne kill her son when she'd been searching for him?" I was revving up again, and Grace pushed my now tepid tea over to hopefully calm me down. "It really comes down to who had the most to lose if what we have laid out here proves true."

Turning back to Grace and my mother, I did the imperial wave to indicate it was more than a rhetorical question.

Grace was first to jump in. "Well, Jake Sr., of course. He could never run for governor if it became known that his son was the result of a gang rape that he participated in at college. Hell, even the hint of it would be fodder for any opponent."

Mother followed quickly. "But could he really kill his son? Everything we've heard indicates he worshipped him, had great plans for him." She took her glasses off and rubbed her eyes. You could tell she was serious since she never wore her specs in public.

"I cannot see it. And I definitely am sure that Cecily couldn't have had anything to do with it. She was totally destroyed by all of this. She is just not that good an actor. She had no clue."

"Exactly." I pointed back to the board. "Wouldn't all Jake's plans crumble if this came out? I think Adrienne was looking to find her son, so any embarrassment or concern would be far outweighed by making the connection."

Absentmindedly rubbing my arm, I put a check by another name on the board. "Patrik Daniel. He's the other person who knew this secret. Remember, Cecily told Mother that it was Daniel's father who told her the story of Senator Jake adopting Bobby from his distant cousin. He could easily have let Patrik know when he started working for the senator."

Looking around at my "class," I continued that thought. "He's been there from the start— he was in the background in the picture you found of the 2001 fraternity class. The one that lists Senator Jake as an alumni advisor to the group. Hell, he was probably in on the rape as well."

Grace had reached over and taken Mother's hand. Her glasses were off again, and she wiped her cheek where a tear had dropped. "That poor child," she whispered.

After a few beats, I cleared my throat and pulled us back to the board. "We already know he doesn't shy away from violence," I said, rubbing my arm again. "And when you think about it, he has as much to lose as Jake does. He's planning on riding Jake's coattails to Washington. This scandal would have totally wiped out those plans."

Mother straightened her shoulders. "Hildy, I think you've done enough. That man has already attacked you once, just for interrupting Jake's party. Can't you get your police chief or someone to look into this now?"

I just shook my head. "Chief West has turned over the investigation to HPD, and I don't think I've endeared myself to Detective Strand. Everyone wants to close this case. They don't want to entertain alternatives."

Walking over to Mother, I picked up her hand and squeezed it. "I promise to be very careful and try not to be alone on campus. I have to find something to put more weight behind this than just conjecture."

Twenty-Six

HARD TO BELIEVE ADRIENNE died almost a month ago. Memorial services held for all parties . . . campus-wide and media-centric for Bobby, quiet and personal for Adrienne. At least the administration was no longer hounding me to get the story off the front page. The media found something else shiny to follow once the possibility of titillating scandal died down. That was the good news. Sadly, I didn't feel any closer to a solution.

Every so often, a blog popped up hinting at deep, dark secrets in Senator Jake's past, but no proof was ever presented, and they faded as well. Probably another flurry when he formally announced a run for the governor's mansion, but quiet until then.

I was having no better luck than the blogs. I believed I knew what really happened. Either Senator Jake or his major-domo Patrik Daniel had killed them both. Jake's alibi seemed to hold up. He was in Austin at a fundraiser. Daniel's calendar also placed him there . . . less than three hours away from the Gulf U campus. Not surprising. He was rarely more than three feet away from Jake.

Chief West told me the time of death was between 5:30 and 6:30. With a fast car, someone could make the drive to Austin in two and a half hours. So it might be possible to get here in the afternoon and make it back to Austin before an eight o'clock banquet. May be tough on Jake . . . someone might miss him. But I bet Daniel could get away with being out of pocket for the afternoon. He was my personal favorite.

As I worked through the day, I'd flip back to the mini-investigation board I'd created in a cloud account so I could access it from home or work. Lost in thought as I stared at my screen, my assistant's tentative knock startled me, and I checked quickly to make sure she couldn't see my computer. I hit the screensaver button as I waved her into my office.

"Yes, Amy. Need something?" I'd pulled a notebook closer, hoping to keep her focus away from my machine.

"Max's office called to confirm your meeting. It's on your calendar, but I wanted to remind you. I put the folder with the information on the new project in your inbox."

I grabbed the blue folder and waved it at her. "Thanks. Just what I needed. Did they say who else was attending? This is a new project in anthropology, right?"

Amy hesitated a moment. "Yes, it's with the person they've brought in temporarily to replace Dr. Harrington. He's from Louisiana Tech. I guess if everyone likes him, he may come on permanently."

"Hmm. I imagine Dr. Minor will be happy if they bring another male professor on board. Definitely make his life easier."

"I guess." Amy stepped back, evidently moving into her office to avoid any possible fallout if I decided to go nuclear.

I chose to ignore her apparent cowardice. She knew me very well. "OK. Thanks for the info. I'll be ready for the meeting."

That gave me only an hour or so to review the background on this new guy and a little on whatever program they wanted to push. It also might take a few moments to get my face working right so I could hide my disgust that Adrienne could be so easily replaced.

I have to get beyond this. Even I know I'm being a bit obsessive, and Max will definitely slap me down if it looks like I have any problem with them bringing in this guy. Louisiana Tech. Really? I shook my head to clear it and opened the folder.

Mardi Gras. The adjunct professor's photo and short bio were attached to the brief on his research. Jason Breaux. Cajun? Attractive photo . . . good for TV.

Who studies the social constructs of local Mardi Gras celebrations in small towns in Louisiana and east Texas? I shook my head at the idea.

OK, definite possibilities for media coverage, especially if there was video to go with it. We were about a week out from Galveston's celebration, so the timing was right. Might even get some national—at least regional—coverage. I could work with that.

The trick would be to compartmentalize his work from Adrienne's position. *I need to deal with this as with any other faculty research. Forget what office he's taking over.* I assumed they had released the crime scene and cleared out all of Adrienne's stuff. Hopefully sent to her aunt.

I read through the brief and then pulled up Breaux's info online. He still had a page on the Louisiana Tech site, which was essentially the printout I had. I checked out his Facebook account, normal stuff, some photos of small-town Mardi Gras, and, after flipping through the usual, a collection of pics with a beautiful blonde woman, his wife or girlfriend. Those pictures stopped showing up about eighteen months ago. No posting explaining a breakup. I should put Amy on it. She could track down anything that existed in the cloud.

My watch buzzed a reminder of the meeting. I gathered my notebook, the file, and my phone and headed to Max's office. As I passed Amy, I leaned in. "Hey, can you do a search on this new guy for me? See what you can find more than his campus info shows."

She nodded, and I went to meet the usurper.

He stood up the moment I entered the room. Max looked at him and then quickly stood up as well. Waving at them to sit, I marched in and took the other seat in front of Max's desk.

Instead of sitting back down, Max walked around his desk to his round worktable and waved us over. "This will be easier to get started." He and Breaux waited until I'd stood up, walked over, and sat back down before taking their own seats.

Well, at least he's polite. I had to secretly grin. *Haven't seen Max in his best manners in a while.*

"OK, Jason, this is Hildy Brentwood. She's one of the best PR people in the business. Hildy, Jason Breaux."

Breaux thrust out his hand, and I shook it quickly.

Max was watching me closely as he continued. "He's here for the rest of the semester . . . maybe longer. We visited when Dr. Minor introduced him to the faculty yesterday, and he told me about his recent work. Mardi Gras. It's almost as big a deal here as in New Orleans. He's looking at how it is celebrated in small towns and rural areas, as well as how it compares to the massive Carnivale celebrations in Rio and other international venues."

I nodded, picking up the blue folder and laying it back down. "So I read. Definite possibilities here with Galveston's celebration just a week away. If we move quickly, we should have enough time to pitch it here and at least regionally. Might even find an opening nationally for a quick piece that would be different from the normal beads and drunks."

Max glared a bit, but Breaux grinned.

"There's a bit more to it than that, but yes, I see where you're going." The man had a dimple in his left cheek that showed when he smiled. And yes, he was absolutely mediagenic. The camera would love all that seal-brown hair, and hazel eyes accented by lush lashes and surrounded by laugh lines. Not to mention his swimmer-lean body.

I gave myself a head-slap for mentally drooling at the guy taking Adrienne's place. "OK, Max, why don't I take Dr. Breaux—"

"Jason."

"Right . . . Jason. Why don't I take Jason down to my office where we can put a plan together and draft a release." I stood up, and the men followed.

Max nodded his blessing to my plan, and we headed back downstairs.

"Hildy . . . can I call you Hildy?"

"Sure," I said without looking at him.

"Great. Hildy, I understand you were a friend of Dr. Harrington—Adrienne. She was a great professional colleague. I'm very sorry for your loss."

That has to be the lamest phrase ever. I always thought police and others who used it routinely should come up with something that felt more real.

I cocked my eyes at him as we walked down the hall. "Yeah, a *loss*. One of my best friends. One of the kindest people I know. She is not a murderer. She did not kill herself or her student . . . no matter what the police and others maintain." I tromped faster.

He kept pace, reaching out to touch my arm, even as I shook him off. He stopped in the middle of the hall. I'd outpaced him and stopped a few feet ahead.

"I guess it sounds lame, but I am truly sorry. I have a hard time believing the Adrienne I knew would ever do something so horrific. It makes no sense. We cowrote a paper a few years ago looking at the customs of Central American peoples compared to rural Louisianans. There were surprising connections." Rubbing his hand through his hair, he'd gotten my attention and continued. "Doesn't matter. We worked pretty closely for the past semester. She visited me in Ruston, and we did some field work in the area where Texas, Louisiana, and Arkansas converge. I was set to join her dig in Costa Rica last December, but we had a COVID scare on campus so I backed out."

"I was on that dig. So was Bobby . . . the kid she's accused of killing. I swear there was nothing going on there. He was her student assistant and that was it." I stared at Breaux until he nodded.

We headed to my office, and I invited him in and closed the door. "She didn't do this. She wouldn't."

"Anybody looking at other possible solutions? Any other candidates?"

Shaking my head, I answered. "Only me. I mean only me trying to find another answer. As much as I loved Adrienne, she didn't suffer fools gladly. There are a few people who were not that upset to see her gone."

Waving him to the table under the window, I grabbed my laptop and set up next to him. With a brief shake of my shoulders, I pulled us back to the task at hand. "Enough of that for the moment. Let's focus on your story. What do you have that we can use visually? Photos? Video? Do you have an article recently published in an academic journal? Any publishing embargoes or restrictions on a current article? I know some journals don't like seeing information on a project appearing in the general media before they publish the official research."

He waited for me to run down. His quirky grin acknowledged my deluge of questions.

"In order . . . yes, yes, yes, and no. I have both film and video. My article is scheduled to appear in the March issue of the *Journal of Socialomics*. It will upload this week . . . twenty-five thousand readers. I'll get you an advance copy. We can do regular media starting Thursday."

Typing quickly on the file I'd already opened for the project, I looked at a possible timeline for release. "That'll work. If you can forward the pics and video and the article, I can get a writer assigned to draft a release for your review. Nothing will go out without your signed approval. Do you have your class schedule yet? I need to get your availability for interviews for the timeline."

He pulled out his phone and accessed his calendar. "I'm starting classes on Monday. Hope to leave Tuesdays and Thursdays open for writing and office hours, so classes set for Monday, Wednesday, and Friday at 10:00, 1:30, and 3:00."

I plugged that into the timeline. "Any other obligations? Family? Girlfriend?"

His smile almost split his face. "Nope. New in town. No affiliations . . . yet."

A shiver ran down my spine, which I quickly shook off. *Not appropriate.*

"Got it. If you can get me your material, we should have a draft for you to review late tomorrow. Renee covers social sciences, so she'll work with you on this. She'll call you after lunch to set up an interview." I stood up and held out my hand. "Welcome to Gulf U. I know this is probably not the way you would have wanted to join us."

Standing as well, he nodded.

"But, nonetheless, we look forward to working with you."

Taking my hand and holding it a few beats longer than necessary, he replied, "In that vein, and seeing as how I really know very few people, would you like to join me for lunch at the campus café? You could fill me in on all the campus politics."

My calendar miraculously showed me free for once, so I nodded. "Sure. Give me a few minutes to get this started, and we can head over to the café. Food's OK. Not anything to write home about, but it will do in a hurry."

We walked briskly across the campus to the food service areas. Eating options had definitely improved since I was in school. As had most everything else, if I were honest about it. The Campus Food Court had outlets for designer coffee, pizza, tacos, chicken in all forms, burgers, salads, stir-fry, cafeteria fare, a small bakery, and an ice cream parlor.

I pulled out my staff ID and credit card as we grabbed trays and silverware. We both drifted to the stir-fry vendor. I ordered chicken and green beans, and he got Thai curry with extra hot sauce. No doubt the creole upbringing allowed for the chili tolerance.

Blessedly, the university set aside an "adult" area for faculty and staff to eat, a bit distanced from the *Sturm und Drang* of the general student grazing area. As we walked behind the sliding wall, the noise level dropped at least twenty decibels. With barely raised voices, we could have a conversation.

"So—"

"So—"

We stepped on each other's line.

I raised my hand and started again. "I don't mean to pry. OK, I probably do mean to pry. But I'm curious. What brings you to Gulf State University? Aren't you a tenured professor at Louisiana Tech?"

He crunched an egg roll and smiled. "Tenured, yes. Happy, not so much. I lost someone a few years ago and found I couldn't seem to move on living and working in all the places we'd been together. Seemed the right time to head off and try to reinvent myself. I was really sad to hear about Adrienne, but this looked like a good place to start the rehabilitation of my life."

My eyebrows met in the middle of my face as I struggled to keep from lashing out.

Apparently sensing my displeasure, he pushed ahead. "I bet that sounded very opportunistic, and I suppose there might have been some of that there." His hand touched mine and then pulled back. "I admired Adrienne and her work, and we had many intersections. I felt I could help her students complete their work and perhaps help work through whatever Adrienne had in play to finish her own research. I hope she'd approve."

I didn't look at his face, staring instead at the congealing Asian food on my plate. Breaux picked up his chop sticks and began eating. Like it or not, he made sense. Our students should not suffer through all this drama. And he seemed sincere about it. In the old days, I might ask, *WWAD—What Would Adrienne Do?* And I knew the answer was take care of her students first.

Picking at my rice, and not about to embarrass myself with chopsticks, I nodded. "I get it. It would be nice if something good came from all this horror. I'm still not sure how I'm going to prove she didn't do this, while keeping the administration off my back. If you have any suggestions, they'd be welcome."

"Maybe you need a new set of eyes. I'd be glad to give you my reactions to what you have found and what you surmise."

I stared into his eyes and his sincerity came through. "Yeah, maybe. We probably shouldn't talk about this on campus. Are you available to come by tonight so I can lay it out for you? We'll be well-chaperoned . . . my mother and daughter will no doubt insist on joining us. Mother might even cater dinner."

I looked down and most of my stir fry was gone. Breaux had also cleaned his plate, so we gathered our trays and dropped the trash in the container in the center of the room. He decided to take a quick tour of the library, and I was headed back to my office. "Renee will holler in the next hour or two. I've got your office phone."

"Here's my cell number and email. Text is probably the fastest way to find me. I keep my cell phone pretty close. I look forward to hearing from her and working with you on both projects." He flashed his dimple once more and walked toward the library.

I took a few moments to watch him go. Had to admit, his backside was as good as his front. Not the only admirer, I noticed a number of coeds turning as he passed. A definite strong addition to campus life. *Adrienne must have loved working with him.*

I caught myself. He was her replacement. He was here only because she no long was. And at that thought, my rusty libido sank back into its primordial ooze.

I had no reason to be flummoxed. Colleagues came to my house fairly often . . . occasionally . . . well, Adrienne had. So why did I change tops three times? And the good bottle of white I'd put aside for some event or another was just a welcome to the campus. All I'd told Mother and Grace was that someone was joining us for wine and coffee who was interested in what we'd found on Adrienne and Bobby.

The doorbell set Shasta off. I recognized her welcome bark and knew it was Mother with Minuit. The tall black greyhound and short white schnauzer were besties. I imagined Grace would bring Catrina. Grace had formally adopted Adrienne's Russian Blue feline. I was relieved when she didn't change her name to Catsy. Catrina no doubt also breathed a cat sigh of relief. The regal cat was also a favorite of the two dogs. The white, gray, and black beasts would eventually curl up in the fuzzy bed in the corner and look like someone had swirled black ink into white paint. Of course, that was after racing through the house at breakneck speed. Minuit, the retired racer, usually lagged behind the others. Evidently she felt she'd done enough running in her previous life.

By the time I got to the door, Grace was also there, dropping Catrina on the floor before Shasta could grab her tail. "Here, you guys have at it. Go. Wear each other out." Grace brushed the cat hair off her jacket as she threw it over the chair near the door.

Mother unwrapped the cashmere scarf and pulled off the matching wool coat. She was in her version of casual wear—long white angora sweater, peg-leg black pants, and short black boots. Grace and I were both in jeans, though my long tunic was a step up from my usual T-shirt with a message.

"So exactly who is coming by?" My daughter gave me a hard stare as she shifted away from the opening into the den. The animals made the tight turn and headed toward the dining room.

I'd already set up my copy of the murder board in the living room and waved my family into the chairs. Stalling a bit, I asked if they wanted wine or anything to drink and put a plate of cheese and crackers on the sofa table.

Mother was looking at me with eyes narrowed, and I folded. "Right. The faculty member who is taking Adrienne's classes arrived today from Louisiana Tech. He's a folklorist and cultural anthropologist who worked with Adrienne in the past."

"Jeez. They've already replaced her? Doesn't that make you crazy?" Grace stood up and then plopped back onto the couch and reached for a cracker.

"I know, it feels weird. But the students need an instructor, and Jason Breaux was available. We're going to work on one of his projects dealing with Mardi Gras in small towns. But that's not the point. We were talking about Adrienne, and he can't believe she'd hurt anyone either. I told him what we were doing offline, and he asked if he could help. Or at least give us a new perspective on it. He should be here in a few minutes." I poured two glasses of wine and put one in front of Mother.

As if on cue, the doorbell rang again, and two dogs raced into the room. Shasta again sounded off, but this time in her I-don't-know-this-person-and-am-ready-to-chew-ankles voice. Minuit was just there for support, standing over her short friend with a big grin on her face. Catrina sauntered in behind them, clearly victorious in the footrace.

"OK, OK. Relax, everyone. Shasta, knock it off. Grace, can you round the dogs up and get them in the backyard. The last thing I need is for Shasta to take a chunk of his ankle."

Grace picked up Shasta, and the troops followed to the back of the house.

After ensuring the house was now ankle safe, I opened the door. "Jason. Please, come in. I've banished the beasts outside for our sanity. I'll take your coat. Come meet the human members of my family."

Grace reappeared as we moved away from the door. I dropped his coat on the chair in the corner.

"Mother, Grace . . . this is Dr. Jason Breaux. As I mentioned, he's joined the faculty for the rest of the semester. Jason, my family . . . my mother, Victoria, and daughter, Grace."

His Southern accent slightly more pronounced, Jason walked over to Mother and gave a very slight bow. "Mrs. Brentwood, it is truly a pleasure. I must admit, when Hildy mentioned you were going to be here tonight, I had to do a quick look. Your work with the city foundation speaks to your commitment to Houston and to the next generation."

Grace grinned at her grandmother, who appeared speechless at the moment.

Jason turned his attention to my daughter with a quick handshake. "First, may I call you Grace? I've had a chance to check out your blog and podcast work for the *Morning News*. Very impressive."

"I appreciate the kind words," she said as she released his hand. "Welcome to Houston, Dr. Breaux."

"Call me Jason. Please. I am grateful to be included in your project."

He moved to the chair that faced the whiteboard. His eyes moved from us to focus on the board. "My, you are indeed deep into your work here."

I walked over with the wine. "This is a pretty good sauvignon blanc, if you'd like, or I have coffee, soft drinks, water."

"Wine, please. And I'd love to hear what all of this means and how I might be able to help." His eyes traced the names, pictures, red and black lines connecting everything, and dotted lines for suppositions (far more of those than we needed.) "This looks very familiar. I use this same diagram system when I outline a book."

A little wine splashed out of his glass as I overpoured. "Oops, sorry. You startled me. I didn't realize you were an author—your bio didn't include that. You mean something in addition to your academic writings?"

"Mysteries. I use a pseudonym. Popular fiction doesn't get you tenure and can be a deterrent. J. Nash Fontenot at your service." He bowed deeply. "I've written a few mysteries set in the bayous of Louisiana. You'd be surprised at how many folks can get themselves killed in the swamps of alligator country."

He took a sip of wine. "Actually, I got interested in small-town Mardi Gras while doing research for my last Sheriff Beau Broussard book."

Grace bounced in her chair. "Oh, I've read those books. They are great fun. Quirky characters, and doesn't he have a pet gator?"

Jason grinned. "He's not actually a pet—more a tenant, living near the dock."

Catrina had chosen her spot for the night. She circled around and curled up in Jason's lap. He gave her a long rub from ears to tail, and her purr almost drowned out our conversation.

I decided it was time to get back to business before my daughter went off into total fangirl. "OK. It's great that you can interpret what we've got spread out over the board. Adrienne had a number of people who might have wanted to do her harm, starting with her ex, who is in serious need of anger-management intervention." Not sure why I felt the need to go into lecture mode, but I was squarely there.

"If I'm reading this correctly, her ex, Darrell Kinkaid, was back in Virginia, teaching at a junior college in Richmond," Jason said.

Tapping the marker on the board, I nodded. "Yes, we've eliminated him . . . and actually have crossed off most of the possibles. Dr. Minor, her chair and nemesis, was giving a paper in Seattle. I was sure there was something going on with Jack Tremayne, the hotshot TV reporter, until he was killed a few weeks ago."

Jason looked over to me. "Killed? Wouldn't that prove Adrienne didn't do this? She was already dead, right?"

Shoulders shrugging, I sighed. "No coincidences, right? Pretty much the rule for every fictional detective, anyway. But not HPD. They've ruled Tremayne's death murder by person or persons unknown. No link to Adrienne's death."

"So who does that leave? And why did they need to remove Tremayne at this point?"

Mother brought Jason a small plate with pear slices, brie, and crackers. She stood over him as he nodded his thanks. She then pointed to our dotted lines leading to the far side of the board. "Senator Jake and his shadow, Patrik Daniel. That's who's left," she said. "They both have alibis . . . fundraising event in Austin . . . but it's less than three hours away and would have been possible with planning."

Jason looked around the room, petting the cat for another round of purring. "Do you really think Jake would kill his son?"

"That's why we're leaning toward Daniel. He could have been out of pocket for the time needed to drive to Houston, kill Adrienne and Bobby, and get back to Austin."

Jason looked about to rise, but Catrina dug her claws into his leg. Dropping back into the chair, he pushed his hand through his hair. "OK, I can see your reasoning of why the other possibilities might have it in for Adrienne and/or Bobby—though I don't quite see Tremayne's motive yet. But why would Jake or his minion want to get rid of the professor, let alone the Jake heir?"

I left the board and poured myself more wine, adding more cheese and crackers to the small plate. Sitting down next to Grace on the couch, I pushed her over with my hip to make room. "It's a convoluted tale going back to Adrienne's college days. Her aunt broke a long silence to tell me about Adrienne being raped the start of her junior year at Virginia. Fraternity party gone very wrong. Pregnant, she gave up the baby and later finished her degree at Virginia Tech."

Stopping for a breath and a bite of brie, I stood up and began to pace around the room. "It looks like Bobby decided to check out Ancestors.com on a bet and discovered a familial connection to his professor. We found the report from the website in his trash. Adrienne had posted her DNA information on the site. She'd asked a friend about the best way to track down an adopted person, and that was one suggestion."

Mother raised her hand. My lecture mode was working. "Hildegard, a quick question. Did Ancestors also flag the DNA match to Senator Jake? That might have set him off."

Grace jumped in before I could. "Actually, Grand, Senator Jake would have had to enter his DNA on the site and give permission for them to share it."

I took the reins again. "No way would the senator want his DNA out on a website. I sincerely doubt if he had any idea that Bobby was trying to find his birth mother. The damage was already done by the time he found out."

I waved my red marker to get us back on track. By then I'd made two circuits around my small living room, getting more wound up at each pass. "Grace did her magic online and found information and photos on the fraternity. Seems law alumnus Robert Jake and his best friend's son Patrik Daniel, now the senator's chief of staff, were members of that fraternity. The dotted line represents our conjecture that they were involved in the gang rape and cover-up. Senator Jake could be Bobby's birth father, but Mrs. Jake is definitely not his birth mother."

Mother took over the story. "I visited with Cecily Jake recently, and she admitted Bobby was adopted privately. Essentially, her husband brought him home one day . . . kind of like adopting a puppy. 'Hey, honey, guess what I got for you?'"

I picked up the tale again. "And here's where a good dose of coincidence does occur. Twenty years later and halfway across the country, Jake finds his son's birth mother teaching him and not recognizing her own son. He's about to announce a run for governor. Not the best time to be faced with proof of a son born out of rape."

Still petting the contented feline, Jason crunched a cracker. "So you believe Adrienne was the target and Bobby got in the way?"

"Yeah, possibly. Or, if Daniel took this on his own, he might have seen a benefit in getting rid of the troublemaking son who was pushing opioids on campus and had just found his birth mother. Much better to have a candidate with a martyred son."

Gulping down the last of my wine, I dropped back on the sofa. "Just have to prove it."

Lifting Catrina gently and laying her back on his chair, Jason walked up to the chart, staring at each photo. He nodded. "I can see it. It plays out for me, even based on circumstantial evidence and conjecture. May have a couple ways to help."

Grace pushed me over and got up, moving next to Jason at the board. "Really? We're needing to keep this on the down-low to protect Mom's job and to keep them from coming after her. She's already been attacked once."

At that statement, Jason stared at me. Rushing to explain, I spoke quickly, barely breathing between sentences. "I got knocked around a bit by someone searching Adrienne's house. I went over to rescue Catrina there. She was Adrienne's. Evidently, someone also needed to get something from her house. I wasn't really hurt, just bundled into the garage. I was only out a short time."

"And what about your confrontation with Daniel? You still have the bruise on your arm." My daughter sounded fierce.

With a grim look, Jason returned his attention to the board. "We need to find something that proves Daniel was in Houston at the right time. I'm the new guy, so no one should link my questions to Adrienne if I'm careful. I wonder if I could get access to the traffic cameras near campus for that day. Bet a few traffic laws got broken if he was in a hurry."

Jumping up from the couch, I almost shouted. "Oh my God. Of course. We have cameras all around the campus. Chief West might help with that. I imagine he knows I'm still looking into this, but he's a friend so won't call me on it if I keep it low-key. Maybe you could use your author persona to get info from HPD for footage a bit further from the campus. If we/you could get a shot of his car in Houston that afternoon, it might pry the case back open."

He looked at his watch and patted my back. "I do need to get back to my place pretty soon. I have classes to prepare, and I'm still going through Adrienne's lesson plans. If I get any information on this, I'll let you know."

At the door, he turned. "Victoria, Grace. It was lovely meeting you, especially a Broussard fan. Hildy, we'll talk tomorrow about the Mardi Gras story and anything else we can find. I appreciate you all sharing this and trusting me to help. Next time, I'll bring dinner."

"Wow." My daughter fanned her face and grinned at me. "They grow them gorgeous in Louisiana. He could be a real keeper, Ma."

"Hold your jets, my girl." I laughed, though my cheeks were probably a nice pink. "Don't even go there. He's replacing Adrienne. That's all I can see now. But he is going to help . . . with the Adrienne mess, I mean."

Mother and Grace gave me the look as they gathered their coats and pets. "We'll see," was all my mother had to say. "We'll see."

Twenty-Seven

THE MARDI GRAS STORY was approved and ready to run. We'd already gotten interest from two local stations, the *Chronicle* and the *Times-Picayune.* The pitch was ready for the nationals.

Ah, Dr. Breaux. He was very photogenic. Definitely good press from this one, and I had to admit to myself at least that I found him intriguing. Tenured professor, secret mystery writer, undercover investigator. Ticking all the right boxes.

Max popped his head in my door. It wasn't often that he'd leave his lofty floor to make a personal visit. Usually an edict came down, or a summons to the tower.

"Hey, boss. Do you need something?" I pulled a pad and pen over in case I needed to take notes. Not used to doing all that on my phone . . . still preferred the old tried and true method.

"No. No. Just checking in. I know you've had a hard few weeks not even counting your bruises from the attack at Adrienne's house. We appreciate you working with Chief West to move the investigation off campus and to the Houston Police. The focus has shifted, and the university is no longer under the microscope."

He paused, still not fully entering the office. "It looks like Dr. Breaux is settling in. He started his classes yesterday and is already getting rave reviews. Mostly from his female students, if my reports are accurate, but he's winning them all over."

"We're ready to push out the Mardi Gras story with him. He'll be great on camera and for interviews. Renee did a great job on the story—light but still clear it is serious research."

Max looked like he had something else to say. And he did. "I have to admit I was worried that you might have felt it was precipitous to push a story so soon for Dr. Harrington's . . . substitute. Of course, the timing on the subject dictated we move quickly on it. But nonetheless, your professionalism is noted." Max looked relieved that he'd gotten it out without a hiccup.

I took a few seconds to get my voice controlled. "We have to do what's best for our students and the university. This story is interesting, and if we were going to cover it, we couldn't wait. We're good."

As he was about to leave, I added. "By the way, did you know Breaux is also a successful author? Mysteries." Jason hadn't asked me to keep that secret, so I hoped I wasn't overstepping.

Surprise and interest ran across Max's face.

I continued. "Pseudonym. J. Nash Fontenot . . . Sheriff Beau Broussard mysteries, set in Thibodaux, Louisiana, of course. I ordered the first one on my e-reader. I'll let you know how they are. Seems to have a good fan base. Before you get too excited," I warned—a lousy poker player, Max's face always gave him away—"I don't believe he wants his fellow professors to know of his secret life. At least not unless he comes on full-time and has tenure to protect him!"

Looking only slightly disappointed, Max nodded. "Fine. Again, I just wanted to thank you for stepping back and moving on from the sadness and mess."

I hoped my face was better at remaining bland without registering either embarrassment at the unfounded praise or worry that I'd been found out. "No problem. I have plenty to keep me busy."

"Great. Keep up the good work." He moved from the doorway and headed out of our area, stepping to pat a few people on the shoulder as he went by.

I wasn't really lying. I was doing university business during office hours, and everything else at home. That's my story, and I'm sticking to it.

Focusing again on the trail of email messages accumulated overnight, I was just clearing out the junk when my cell began playing the Beatles' "With a Little Help from My Friends." I grabbed it without looking at the display and jumped when Jason Breaux said my name.

"Wow, we were just talking about you and there you are." I might have gushed a bit.

"Great minds," he replied. "I just wanted to thank you again for pushing through my research story. Your writer, Renee, is great to work with. She already has three interviews set for me in the next week." He paused. "So who's the *we* who were talking about me? You and Renee?"

"Earlier, she briefed me on how the story was doing. She liked working with you as well. But I was referring to my boss, Max Levine. He told me you already wowed the female students in your classes, and the guys aren't far behind. Congratulations."

Now he sounded a bit embarrassed. "Really not all that hard. Indiana Jones paved the way for professorial archeologists. I'm just taking it to the next level . . . showing the science behind it all. I must admit, I was worried about moving into Adrienne's space. She always connected well with her students. I'm glad it seems to have passed on to me. Fingers crossed it will hold."

I breathed deeply before the next piece. "I do need to confess that I might have let your fictional life out of the bag. You never said to keep it quiet, and Max was singing your praises and then thanking me for backing away from Adrienne's case, and I just spilled it . . . your novels and pseudonym. Turns out he's read a few and was excited to have a *New York Times*-ranked author on campus, which I must say was more than I knew."

My data dump over for the moment, I took another breath. "I had to parse his appreciation to accept it for my university work and put aside what I'm doing at home. Your alter ego evidently served as a good distraction. I did tell him to keep it quiet, at least until you decide if you are going to stay around past this semester."

"No problem. And so far, I'm feeling properly welcomed. Y'all have gone out of your way to bring me into the campus family. And into your family. I hope I can continue to help with your after-work project." If we'd been on FaceTime, I knew his dimple would be showing.

Shaking my head to get back to business, I jumped back to my job. "So are you just checking in, or do you need something to help with your interviews?"

"I suspect I should save this report for after work. How 'bout I buy you dinner tonight, and I'll tell you what I've found so far. Can I pick you up about 6:30? You need to choose the restaurant since I'm a newbie here. I like about anything, but prefer we go somewhere particular to Houston. Not too fancy so I can wear my teaching jeans."

Choking back a laugh, I nodded and then spoke into the phone with an agreement to meet after work. Hanging up, I tried unsuccessfully to refocus on the reports on my desk. Were we actually flirting? *Wow, it's truly been a long time if I have to think about it.*

Shasta sounded off with her usual warning—high-pitched and frantic. Someone was at the door. I assumed it was Jason, as it was exactly 6:30. Nonetheless, I checked through the window before unlocking the door. Admonishing Shasta to stand down and wait for me, I carefully opened the door and invited him in.

Why do guys look so good in jeans and a pullover? I changed my outfit three times before settling on black skinny jeans and this shimmery tunic in tones of old gold. *I bet he just pulled out the first thing in the closet.*

Keeping a close eye on Shasta standing guard in my favorite chair, we moved into the den. I grabbed her and sat down as Jason took the other reading chair in the room. "Sorry about the noise. She thinks she is a police dog in charge of this block . . . particularly this house. And she isn't around many men, so she does tend to try to herd them with strategic nips on their ankles." I squinted a bit, holding tight to my dog and my nerves. *Did I just screw up this deal? Maybe I should have left her outside again.*

Jason settled back in the chair. "So this is the infamous Shasta. Don't worry. She's just doing her job . . . protecting you. You live alone, so it's really good to have an early warning system." He didn't seem put off by the yapper or the possibility of being herded.

"Non-rawhide chews. Can I offer her one?" Easing himself out of the chair and onto the floor, he picked up the bag with the thin chew strips. "Go ahead, let her go. We're going to get on just fine."

Shaking my head, I relaxed my tight hold but kept a hand on her collar. She looked at me and then at Jason, not sure what to do next.

"Don't look at me," I told her. "I don't know what's happening either. I suggest you try to behave yourself."

Shasta oozed off the chair, much as Jason had. She belly crawled toward him, stopping at his shoes. I was about to tell him to mind his ankles, but a quick glare kept me quiet. He'd left an opening between his legs, holding the thin treats in his lap. It took five minutes, but eventually she had her nose up against his hand. She looked up and gave him her best starved dog stare, willing him to drop the treat for her.

He remained still until Shasta was finally in his lap, curling up for a good snack. His back against the chair, he looped his hand around the dog and lifted them both back into the seat. She didn't even wiggle.

Amazing. A real dog whisperer. Now I'm truly a goner.

I took a deep breath after holding it for some seconds. "Well, that was darn impressive, I must say. I don't think anyone has won her over so quickly and thoroughly."

"The quickest way to get people in small towns to warm to you is to win over their dogs. That was one of the most important things I learned while doing my Mardi Gras research. And it helps that I genuinely like animals, particularly dogs." He was now rubbing her ears and scratching her chest. She was in dog heaven.

"You are just full of surprises, aren't you?" That came out flirtier than I had expected. Toning my voice down, I stood up. "If you can break away from your new conquest, I made reservations for us at seven. It's not far, but we probably should head out."

Shasta grabbed the second treat as he moved, jumping to the floor. She took her prize to the fluffy dog bed in the corner and settled in.

I picked up a crocheted shawl I'd thrown over a chairback. Before I could swing it around my shoulders, Jason touched my hand and took possession. He gently placed it around me and moved me toward the door.

I was glad I hadn't mentioned our meeting to Mother. I'd have had to change my outfit at least five more times if I had. When Grace learned about it, I would swear it was research for the investigation, but it felt more and more like a real date.

Opening the door carefully, making sure Shasta was still in her bed, we moved onto the porch. He pulled his arm from my back and escorted me down the steps to his fire engine-red Mustang . . . all electric. I'd been coveting it since Ford brought it out earlier this year.

As the engine roared, Jason looked over. "So where are we heading? I hope somewhere here in the Heights."

"Not far. Head back to 11th and turn right. It's a new northern Italian restaurant, Trattoria Sofia. Just a few miles down the street. I love their take on caponata. Great pasta and rustic pizza as well. Not warm enough yet to eat on the patio, but the noise level is OK for a conversation in the restaurant."

Ten minutes later, he pulled into the parking lot. We were seated with a glass of wine in minutes. After the usual back and forth over the menu, I totally won with my favorite caponata and margherita pizza.

"I must thank—"

"To be honest—"

We both laughed.

"Ladies first," he said.

"Well, not that important. I guess I wanted to admit that I didn't expect to like you very much . . . what with you taking over my friend's job." He began to respond, and I interrupted again. "No, please. I guess this is kind of an apology for prejudging. I appreciate your willingness to look beyond the headlines and imagine another possibility with me. It means a lot."

He nodded. "I have to say first that you hide your apprehension very well." I shrugged my shoulders with a small laugh. "And remember, I knew and admired Adrienne. I have as hard a time as you do believing she could commit suicide, let alone murder. Hopefully, together we can prove them all wrong."

When the appetizer arrived, we settled for sampling the good food. We waited until we were served the pizza before revisiting the reason for the meeting.

Jason pulled out his phone, tapping on the notes icon. "I visited with Chief West yesterday. Either I'm a lousy James Bond, or he's a great detective, 'cause he wasn't fooled a minute by my excuse for wanting information on the road and parking lot cameras. After first instructing me to tell you to back away, he seemed intrigued by our premise and called up the files. We didn't find any smoking guns like trailing Patrik Daniel down the walkway to the social sciences building at the time of the killings."

He knew how to milk a moment, taking a drink of red wine before finishing. "However, West was able to pull up some of the city's traffic cams, and we found what could be Daniel's black Mercedes SUV running a light on Memorial Drive about five o'clock. For some reason the photo was distorted with only a partial license plate. The driver was wearing dark glasses and a cap, so facial recognition is difficult. West had to concede it was possible that Daniel had lied about being in Austin the entire day."

I was bouncing in my seat as he finished. Grabbing his hand, I barely kept from squealing. "That's fantastic. Can West push it through HPD and get them to take another look?"

Shaking his head, Jason put the phone back in his pocket. "West didn't think it was enough to have them reopen the case. He did promise he would ask around and see if there was anything else he could find. I think that's as good as we're going to get."

No longer hungry, I sat back in the booth. There had to be a way. Maybe it was time to confront Daniel directly. I needed to ponder that before suggesting it to anyone on my team, knowing they'd veto any direct action before I'd get it out of my mouth.

"I'm not sure where to go next." I tried but couldn't keep from sounding as frustrated as I felt. I got a hand pat for that.

Jason waved for the check. "Promise I'll let you know if I think of another possibility," he said. "I can keep asking around in my new guy on the block persona. Someone might have seen something they didn't think important. Never can tell."

I thanked him for dinner and the help as the valet brought his car. I was disappointed that we hadn't gotten further but surprisingly glad we'd gone out. Not sure where that came from, and definitely not reporting that back to the family.

I'd barely fed Shasta and got the first pod of coffee dripped into my cup when rapping on the back door broke the blessed silence of the morning. Grace. Not surprised, and at least she'd waited until we were up.

"Come in, Gracie, it's unlocked," I hollered.

She walked in, heading straight for the coffee. "Mom! You can't just leave your doors open for anybody to wander in. This isn't Smalltown USA or 1950."

Yeah, yeah. Who's the mother here? My inner scold pushed to be unleashed. I waited a beat before answering to keep from going down that impossible rabbit trail.

"Thanks, honey. You are most helpful." Of course, she didn't hear the sarcasm and just smiled her angel smile.

"I'm actually here this early to hear about last night. How was Jason? Have fun? How was the restaurant? Did you invite him in for drinks after dinner?"

I don't think she took a single breath between questions. "Fine, yes, good, no. That answer everything?" I gave her my innocent smile.

"Come on, Mom. I may have to live vicariously through you for the near future, so I want details. Give me the deets, as the kids say today."

"Deets? Really? Do they still say that?" I grinned and dragged out my report. "Not that much to tell you. I enjoyed dinner and getting to know Jason better. And no, I don't think either of us is ready for late night drinks, plus whatever. He was interesting, fun, the perfect gentleman."

I decided to fill her in on the serious part of our conversation. "We talked about Adrienne and the investigation. Chief West let him review the campus traffic and parking cameras, and they might have caught a shot of someone in a car similar to Daniel's just outside the campus."

Grace gulped a swallow of coffee and just avoided choking on the hot drink. "But that's it, right? Proves he was here and not in

Austin the day Adrienne and Bobby were killed. Did West agree to take it to the HPD?"

"He said it wasn't enough. No specific ID on the driver and only a partial plate on the car. West told Jason the HPD wouldn't change their findings on suspicion and conjecture. So we're stuck for the moment." I decided to leave it there.

Staring hard, Grace snorted. "I recognize that look. That's your *I'm going to jump in with both feet and to hell with responsibility or good sense* face, and it worries me."

"You're imagining things. Don't worry, I'm not going to do anything crazy." I hoped I looked as innocent as I sounded.

"I'm not sure we have the same definition of crazy." She gave me her hard look, as if she hoped to see inside my skull.

I pulled her over and gave her a hug. "You worry too much. I'm fine. I've got more than enough work at the school to keep me busy for weeks. Stop hovering. You're like one of those helicopter moms only pint-sized."

She rubbed her hand over her slightly showing baby bump. "Not all that pint-sized at the moment. Consider it good practice."

Finding a possible change of subjects, I jumped in. "Have you decided on whether to find the gender of the baby or stick with your belief she is a girl? And when are you going to tell Brad?" And the volley was successfully launched over the net.

Her hands again going to her middle, Grace smiled. "I go in next week for the next ultrasound, and I'll learn what flavor of kid I'm cooking. I definitely want to know. Brad is still in Brazil on assignment. I think he's headed to eastern Europe next. I won't sidetrack him. He lives for his work. And I'm perfectly capable of raising this child myself... with a little help from you and Grand. We'll be great."

I'd take the win of changing the subject and not push for the father's right to know for a while.

"Want company for the big reveal next week? I have plenty of comp time and would love to be with you for that."

She bounced on the stool and clapped. "Perfect. How 'bout if you bring Grand as well? We can celebrate with brunch afterward. Tuesday, 10:00 a.m. We'll be at the women's pavilion at Texas Children's. Supposed to get a tour of the birthing unit as well. Baby all the way!"

"Perfect. Mother would skin us if we didn't bring her. An all-day outing. Maybe we can work in a mani-pedi as well. Consider it a date." I gently touched her belly and grinned.

"Now get yourself in gear. You may be able to work in your pj's at home, but I have an office to get to and real work to do."

Twenty-Eight

ADRIENNE'S DEATH HAD OFFICIALLY dropped from the mainstream news. The university was happy . . . it was long off the front page. HPD was happy . . . they'd closed their case. Senator Jake was happy . . . the tragic loss of his son had gained him innumerable pity points in his quest for the governor's mansion. And somewhere a murderer was happy . . . he'd gotten away with it.

Routine had set back into my work. Jason's Mardi Gras story hit national online and print media, keeping him and Gulf U in the positive spotlight through Mardi Gras week. We were gearing up for the spring festival and opera performance, and I'd assigned Renee to develop an online outreach for Giving Tuesday with a goal of increasing online giving by five percent.

Non-job also had returned to our definition of normal. Mother and I took Grace to her ultrasound appointment. Another generation of Brentwood women would join us in about six months. Jason and I had connected a couple of times. Another restaurant and a late visit to Anderson Fair for music. He loved singer/songwriters almost as much as I did. And Shasta never changed, lording it over a square block area around our bungalow.

However, my frustration with finding an answer for Adrienne was bordering on nuclear. We were officially at a loss. All my research and prognostications had led me to believe that Patrik Daniel killed both Adrienne and Bobby. He killed to protect his senator boss, whether Senator Jake was involved or not. All the other suspects were either cleared or dead. But conjecture didn't come close to proof. I had nothing but my conviction. And I was not supposed to have even that.

At least Max was no longer checking in daily on my Nancy Drew tendencies. Nothing to see. Nothing to do.

Those days, I seemed to keep up with the movement of the large clock on my office wall. For the first time in my career, I shut down after nine or ten hours, rather than pushing into the witching hour—reflection of having a personal life again and, I had to admit, being locked in a repetitive loop at work. There was only so much change in the academic/events calendar each year. We were approaching March Madness, and the Gulf U basketball team was teed up for a run for the NCAA title.

Thank God the sports media office handles all the teams. Not the first time I'd evoked that prayer during my career. We were responsible for the student and community reaction to the games and any rallies on or off campus to cheer on the team. Every school whose team had won the national championship in the past saw a huge bump in both donations (not just to athletics) and in enrollment, both quantity and quality. Success definitely bred success.

Computer was off. I'd picked up my notebook and cell, dropping both into my briefcase/purse slung over my shoulder. I was almost out the door when the phone rang. Everyone else was already gone. I blamed my job on my inability to leave a phone to ring itself to voice mail. What if it was the president? Or my contact at CBS? Or Publisher's Clearinghouse?

Dropping my bag back on the desk, I snatched the receiver before the fourth ring. "Public Relations. Hildy Brentwood speaking. How can I help you?"

"Great. I was afraid I'd miss you and was about to pull out my list with your cell phone number."

"Chief West? Is there a problem? Do you need something quickly?" Except in dire emergencies, I usually got word of problems through Max or the president. Last time West called me directly was to bring me in after Adrienne's death.

His voice seemed calm, but then that was his default mode. I knew my voice had moved toward the shrill range as I stopped to breathe.

"No. Not an emergency per se." He paused a beat. "It's just, I've been thinking since your friend Dr. Breaux and I reviewed the traffic cams. I think I've found something. Something that might impact the ruling on Dr. Harrington and Bobby Jake's deaths."

I sat down hard, and then, as his words sunk in, I began bouncing in my chair. "What? A clue? It must be major if you think it could change HPD's verdict." I was already imagining a number of scenarios that could be playing out.

West broke into my mind games. "It might be nothing, but worth checking. I know, despite the administration's admonition, you're still trying to find another answer to their deaths. You interested in meeting me in the racquetball courts so I can show you something I've found?"

"Racquetball courts? You mean the ones in the tunnels under the library? What could you have found there?" I was already gathering my stuff again, ready to head out.

"It's easier to show you than trying to explain it all. Meet me there in fifteen minutes. I can have you out and on your way quickly after that." He didn't even hint at whatever evidence he'd uncovered.

I was desperate and quickly agreed. "Yes, I can meet you there in fifteen minutes or so. Chief, I thought you didn't believe me nor approve of my investigating?"

Now he sounded impatient. "I just want to find justice for them and for Gulf U. See you in fifteen."

My brain was doing cartwheels. Locking the office, I headed out. The library was just across the quad. It was six o'clock, and the winter sky had already darkened. Lights marked the path across the park. I pulled my cell phone out of my bag as I fast-walked down the sidewalk. Jason was my last call, so redial started ringing. His voice mail instructed me to leave a message.

"Hey Jason, Hildy here. Chief West called and said he found something that might clear Adrienne. I'm headed to the tunnels to meet him. I know you want answers as much as I do, so if you get this in the next ten minutes, you can join us at the racquetball courts under the library. If not, I'll fill you in later. Bye."

Before dropping my phone in my jacket pocket, I hit the record app so I wouldn't have to take notes. It would be easier to keep the information West had on my phone for reference and to share with Jason and others. I headed into the library to find answers.

I didn't think I'd beat West to the underground courts, so wasn't surprised to see him as I rounded the second turn. It had taken a few minutes to get the storm door opened at the base of the library's basement stairs. It was like walking through a submarine, stepping high to move from one room to the next with watertight doors between sections. The university flooded about ten years before when the tunnels were open to every major building. The entire electrical grid, including computers and HVAC, was destroyed. Now, in the event of a major storm, the watertight doors would be activated and locked down. Houston had no shortage of water emergencies, so this system had proved invaluable in the past.

It was still officially winter, and the relatively minor cold front sitting over Houston left the tunnels damp and chilly. I shivered as I approached West.

He was staring at the wall. "I knew you couldn't resist an opportunity to find answers. You couldn't just let it drop. Mourn your friend and move on." He turned, raising his hand and pointing a gun at me. "I never wanted to harm you, but you were starting to move in the wrong direction. As long as you focused on Dr. Harrington and who would want to harm her, I felt pretty safe."

Backing up, I looked around the empty room, hoping to find someone else. He couldn't be speaking to me. We'd worked together for more than ten years. We were friends and colleagues.

I shifted to my left as he pointed that way with the gun. As I moved out of the doorway, he pulled it shut, sealing the room so no light or sound would escape.

"What the hell, Chief? What are you doing? Why?" I was sure my voice would come out as a squeak but managed to hold steady.

He just stared at me, shaking his head. "I like you, Hildy. You're feisty. But you wouldn't let it alone. And you were running out of suspects for Harrington's murder. I was sure you'd turn to Bobby next. I couldn't let you do that."

I must have looked confused, because he shrugged and continued. "Can't figure it out? You're the smart one. The Nancy Drew wannabe. Surely you can play out this scenario."

And the other shoe dropped. "You're the inside man. So it was true. Bobby was dealing drugs. You're Bobby's supplier. He had to get it from someone, but I never connected the dots to you."

West seemed a bit sorry but resolute as I continued spinning my new yarn.

"But I'm confused. If you needed to end your business relationship with Bobby, why bring it back to campus? He could have had an accident. Or an accidental overdose somewhere away from campus. Why bring Adrienne into it?"

My scenario-building seemed to settle me. At least I no longer heard my teeth chattering. And I hadn't fainted—one point for Hildy. Maybe I'd get answers before I joined my dead friend.

"Stop, Hildy. Before we go any further, hand over your cell phone."

I dug around the bottom of my satchel and pulled out my Google Pixel—the one Gulf U upgraded for me the previous month.

West took it and stomped his work boot on the screen.

"That was state property. They'll charge you." Wow, I still had my snark. I was counting on my poker face to keep my personal iPhone in my pocket away from him. Mental fingers crossed that the recorder was still working.

West looked up after smashing my phone and continued answering my question without a lost beat. "I hadn't intended to

. . . you know, kill her. Really." He looked beyond me for a moment. "I had a meeting set with Bobby. He was going wild. Pushing to embarrass his father for his twentieth birthday with a crazy drug event. I couldn't let that go."

My inner journalist was thankfully still in control. "How did you find out about Adrienne and Bobby . . . that he was her son?"

"Well, Tremayne, of course. He had files and clips and a birth certificate. He'd just made the connection to Adrienne. He'd have blackmailed her and/or the senator if I hadn't intervened. I was doing the world a service."

I didn't find it funny, but West seemed to as he continued. "Bobby was entirely gobsmacked when he found out Adrienne was his mother. He was headed there when I learned about his party planning." He brought his focus back to me.

"Why Tremayne? I don't believe in coincidences, so his murder has to be connected somehow. What did he have on you?"

"I don't intend to be the *villain* who spends thirty minutes explaining how and why. Suffice it to say that slimy blackmailer got what he deserved. I'm not the only one glad to see the end of him."

"OK. Then explain why you tore up Adrienne's house and attacked me? What were you looking for?" I had to keep him talking while I tried to think of a way out.

"Wasn't me. Probably somebody from Jake's camp trying to find the DNA information on Harrington. Or it could have been a random break-in, as HPD insisted." He moved closer, and I stepped back.

West shook his shoulders and steadied the gun. "Enough talking. Hildy, you give me no choice. You just couldn't take a hint. Without your interference, this would have gone away weeks ago."

He motioned with the gun to head through the door at the back of the courts. "We're going to walk through the tunnels to the deserted leg where the old computer servers were before Tropical Storm Allison flooded the campus. Deserted now since they abandoned that section and moved the backup system to the top of the library. I imagine people will wonder and even search for you. I'll lead that search to assure them you must have pissed off the wrong people and paid the price. I promise I'll be as sad as anyone else when we don't find your body. Now move."

I took a few tentative steps. I needed to stall, hoping for a miracle. "Chief, you don't need to do this. Hell, until I saw your gun, I had no idea you were anything but what you said. You've been hiding behind your badge since you got here from LA."

He pointed the gun at the door again and then back to me. "Not that it's any of your business, but I left LA before it blew up. I had my sales crew at USC and was building my retirement account to support my future on a sandy beach somewhere. Blame it on a nosy detective-partner, kinda like you, actually. She began asking questions, so I retired early. Houston seemed a good solution. No connections. Getting the job on campus meant I could keep my eye on the sales team." He prodded me in the back as I slowed down. "Keep moving."

"How'd you figure out it was Tremayne who was blackmailing you? Did he know about the drugs, or did he find out about the killing?" Could I keep him distracted enough to veer off into one of the tunnels ahead?

"He'd gotten to Bobby and started after me. Another reason Bobby had to go. Didn't take much to figure out who was trying to bust into my business. Shit, I'm a detective, remember. Tremayne was an amateur. I left him at the bar where I failed to deliver his blackmail money. He wasn't going to need it. I took his keys and dropped in to make sure he didn't have anything in his files. I clearly was not his first victim. Once I found his files, I discovered a wealth of information on some very interesting people. I might spin off a side business. Hate to let some of those folks off the hook. Of course, I left enough information to lead the police to believe one of his other blackmail victims had killed him."

I'd slowed down as he bragged about his success. "I still don't get how Adrienne got pulled into all this?"

"Bobby again, of course. When I caught up with him outside her office, she thought I was arresting him for something and came out to help. In the process, Bobby confessed I was his dealer. I pushed them back into her office before he attracted more attention. She went for an antique dagger in her bookcase. A much better weapon than a noisy gun. Bobby jumped in as we wrestled with it. I nicked him in the shoulder and then pulled back and caught him in the chest. Before she could call out, I rammed the knife in her gut. My luck held, and she grabbed the hilt as she fell. And just like that, we had murder-suicide."

Not much more to the story. I needed to act soon. With nothing to lose, I suddenly stopped, causing him to bump up against me. I pivoted, stomped on his foot, and jammed my knee into his groin. As he folded in on himself, I took off running around the corner and through the next submarine door. There had to be an entrance into a building somewhere. I'd gained less than a minute before West recovered enough to curse loudly and head after me.

Got it. The tunnel under the social sciences building. Full circle.

I was gasping as I grabbed the door and headed up the stairs. Would he risk using his gun as we moved into the building and out of the sound-resistant tunnels? I had to get to people . . . somewhere public.

Running upstairs while pushing the connect button on an iPhone is at least as hard as it sounds. But desperation and a bit of luck were in my favor. The last call I'd made was to Jason. *Please God, let him answer.*

"Jason. Jason, help!"

"Hildy?"

Oh, thank God. "It's West, Chief West. He has a gun. I'm in Masterson Hall—social sciences. Hurry, call HPD—not campus cops." I had to stop talking before I passed out. West was just behind me. With a final burst, I pushed open the door to the foyer right into the night class student shuffle. At least forty students and professors wandered across the building's first floor, trying to get to their classrooms before the hour.

I prayed West hadn't morphed into a mass murderer who would blast through dozens of people to get to me. *Yes.* I recognized a colleague at the elevators and ran toward him. As the doors opened, Jason walked off, grabbing me. He pulled me behind his back as he scanned the room for West. I couldn't see him either. Had he moved back into the tunnel?

Jason kept his arm around me as we moved to the side of the room. I was breathing heavily from fright and exertion. He moved me to a bench by the window. "Sit. Breathe. I called the cops, and they'll be here soon." His hand rubbed up and down my arm.

"I've got it. I've got it all. I recorded him. He's a major drug dealer and has been for years, even in LA. Bobby was screwing up the deal, so he eliminated the problem. Adrienne was just in the wrong place. She tried to protect Bobby and died for it." I finally took a breath.

As I looked up, Detective Strand entered the building, followed by two uniformed policemen. She scanned the foyer and then came over to our bench.

"Ms. Brentwood. Dr. Breaux. Mind telling me what this is all about?" I was amazed that Strand had come herself.

Pulling my phone from my pocket, I handed it to her. "Here. This is the easiest answer. Replay the last recording. It seems our Chief West has been running a very lucrative side business . . . one leading to murder." I was running out of steam but didn't want to go home to an empty house.

"OK, Hildy." Detective Strand dropped my phone in an evidence envelope. Patting me on the shoulder, she looked anxious to join the chase. "We'll take it from here. You can come to the HPD office tomorrow and file your formal report. Do you have someone you can stay with tonight until we have this sorted out?"

"I guess I could stay with my mother." I mentally cringed. *Would Jason be willing to stay over until West was in custody?*

Strand seemed to think we had it all sorted out and joined her colleagues as they started the search.

Jason and I left the building as quickly as possible. "You OK to drive?" he asked as we walked to my car.

"Sure, I guess so. Not as sure about going to my house alone."

Jason shook his head. "That won't be happening while West is still out there. Consider me a new short-term roomie. Shasta and I get along fine. She can share the couch. My car is in the faculty lot. Lock yourself in, and I'll swing around to follow you home."

So much for worrying about how to move ahead with Jason. We were moving to stage two immediately. I whispered a quiet bravo into the universe and followed his red Mustang into the Heights.

Twenty-Nine

THE CARAVAN FINALLY ARRIVED at my house. Not surprisingly, Mother and Grace were in front, sitting in my mother's Lincoln. I could thank the broadcast and social media for blasting out my rescue before I had a chance to call home. My bad. I should have sent a text that I was OK before they heard anything. Four car doors opened simultaneously. We all crammed onto the porch as I searched for my key. At least my outside lights provided necessary illumination.

My hand shook as I tried to get the key in the lock. Finally, we were in. I reached the keypad to shut off the alarm. Shasta bumped me on the leg and then jumped up on Jason begging for attention. *Hey, ever heard of loyalty?* I pulled on her collar to get her back on the floor.

"OK, everyone find a seat. Coffee? Something stronger?" I looked at my family, including Shasta and Jason, and waited.

Mother led the blast. At her steely eyed look, I dropped onto the couch. "Well, girl, I'm glad to see you are all in one piece. Could not really tell based on the TV coverage. What the hell were you thinking, going into a closed place . . . underground of all things . . . with a potential killer?"

I straightened up and shot back. "First of all, I went down there to meet a supposed friend. Someone I'd trusted and worked with for years. A police officer. I guess I'm not such a great detective, since he took me totally by surprise."

Jason interrupted. "Don't sell yourself and your fellow *detectives* short. You'd analyzed all the information, clues, suppositions on the most likely suspects. West was never on anyone's radar . . . neither the pros nor the amateurs."

He bumped his knee against mine in a show of solidarity. "Mrs. Brentwood, you should be proud. Hildy kept her cool when she could have totally folded. Her recording of West's bragging confession will lead to his conviction. And she kept him talking long enough to get herself away from him and for the police to reach the building. My favorite part is that she used the training she learned from West's self-defense class to get away." I'd evidently shared that tidbit in my fog as we waited for HPD.

Jason continued. "HPD has a manhunt in process. Roads and transportation options monitored, warrants for his home and office, review of his time in LA. They'll find him and lock him up. And don't worry. I'll be sleeping on the couch until he is safely in custody."

By this time we were sitting together hip to knee, and it felt great. My post-adrenaline decline was replaced by a growing connection. And despite my long trek through the dating desert, I think there was even a bit of sexual tension with Jason. I just had to get Mother and Grace through their angst and out of my house.

"The long and short of it, which I imagine is still being kept under wraps by the police, is that West was operating a major drug distribution system through the campus. He was doing it in LA before rumors started there. He decided Houston would be a safer venue, and our opening for a new police chief was the perfect solution."

Grace was taking notes on her cell for her Dallas newspaper blog.

Nice to have her scoop the local media with her insider access, I thought.

"Bobby was the real target. He became a liability when he identified Adrienne as his birth mother and planned to go after his father with an embarrassing drug giveaway event at his twentieth birthday party. Adrienne was just collateral damage, according to West. Wrong place, wrong time. I need to call Angela Johnson, Adrienne's aunt. Like us, she never believed her niece was a killer. She'll be relieved we've now proved her right."

My hand reached over and lightly touched Jason's knee. *Time to move Mother out.* My libido was pushing hard against my need to lecture.

"OK, one more question, and then I'm going to close down. I think my body is reaching the post-adrenaline droop."

Grace jumped in. "Tremayne. Where does he come into all of this?"

"I actually know the answer to that one. West told me he was being blackmailed about the drug dealing. He tracked it back to Tremayne, who also had recorded him on his phone going into Masterson Hall at the time Adrienne and Bobby were killed. So he took care of the problem. Seems Tremayne supplemented his income with a fairly robust sideline of blackmail and protection. You paid to keep your secrets off his news program. West discovered quite the cache in Tremayne's home. Detective Strand should find some interesting opportunities once she catches up with West."

I stood up ready to shoo my family to the door. "I need to crash now. I feel safe with Jason on the couch and Shasta ready to sound off if anyone steps foot on her castle grounds."

Picking up her purse, Grace dropped her cell back in the front pocket. "OK. I have one last question—who attacked you at Adrienne's? That doesn't seem connected to the drug operation."

My arm snaked around her waist as I walked with her to the door. "Oh yeah. You're right. That wasn't West. I think I got that right. Daniel and Senator Jake were responsible. Evidently searching for Adrienne's DNA information and the letter from Ancestors.com. I mentioned that to Detective Strand, and she agreed to look into the attack as a separate case. My guess is if she can match their DNA to any of the damage done at the house, there won't be any governor's announcement in the near future."

Family out the door, I was fading fast and still had many things to ponder—not the least of which was my new connection to Jason. I'd also disobeyed a number of directives and orders from my boss and Gulf U's administration. Not sure how Max or President Murphy would take it now that I'd brought the story back to campus. Sure, I finally identified the killer. Cleared the reputation of my dead friend and colleague. Shut down a major drug ring on campus. All of which would bring more negative coverage to the university. The scariest thing to ponder was where Chief West was. When would they find and arrest him? When could I feel safe again in my home, my university?

I pulled a pillow and quilt from the closet and dropped them on the couch. "Jason, I'm heading for bed before I drop. Feel free to get anything you need. I do have a few things in the kitchen, and you're welcome to any of it. Just keep them away from Shasta. She's an expert beggar."

Laughing, he pulled me into a hug. "I'm good to go. You try to get some sleep."

I washed off my makeup. Much of it had run down my face in my terror and exertion. As tired as I felt, I hesitated before climbing into bed. Would I be haunted by my harrowing time with West? *Maybe if I concentrate on our success in clearing Adrienne, I'll dream of her and our good times.*

Just as I finally closed my eyes, fingers crossed for dreamless sleep, my Apple Watch buzzed me with a call. Detective Strand had my iPhone, but I was still hopelessly wired in by my watch these days.

"Huh. Yeah. Sorry, you caught me drifting off. Who's calling?" My voice was registering in its deepest tone, too tired to sound perky.

"Hildy. It's Detective Strand."

My eyes popped wide open. Jerking up in the bed, I brought the small watch closer to my ear so I could hear every word. "What? Have you found his trail? Are we safe here?"

"Yes, you're totally safe. We cornered Chief West at a lake house his ex-wife got in their divorce. He evidently still had a key and was hiding out there. I can't tell you much, except he didn't surrender when we approached him. He looked me straight in the eye and pulled his gun out. I fired first, and he dropped. He wasn't even wearing a vest. It was a righteous shoot, but it will be with me for a long time. I swear he held his shot. He wanted to end it this way. Suicide by cop."

I could almost see her shoulders tighten as her voice dropped with that last line. "I'm sorry it ended that way, though I'm glad it will put the final note in the file. I really appreciate you calling to let me know. And I appreciate you and the HPD moving so quickly once this broke. It could have ended very badly if you hadn't stepped up. I'll be in tomorrow to finalize my statement for your files, and thanks again for the notice."

As Strand disconnected, I swung my legs over the edge of the bed. I should probably tell Jason the danger was over. He no longer needed to provide security. He could head home to his own bed. *Or I could wait till morning. He's already tucked in and probably snoring. No need to disturb him now.* My thoughts swirled. I had to admit it was very nice having him just a room away. Without the threat of reprisal from West, it might have been months before we reached this level.

My earlier plan to focus on Adrienne, and our friendship was the perfect end to a harrowing day . . . month. I drifted off to Survivor's iconic song "Eye of the Tiger." The anthem Adrienne and I adopted, along with Mica and Abby, our girl gang group—plus newest members Grace and Mother.

We'd survived and proved the fight was worth it. And I would continue to prevail, no matter what happened with Gulf U and Max. Not that I was worried. I couldn't imagine the shit storm that would happen if I got fired over this. Whatever. I'm a survivor . . . and soon to be a grandmother and maybe even a girlfriend. Can't get better than that.

The End

Author's note: If you enjoyed Hildy's adventure in *Deliver Us from Evil . . . and the Six O'Clock News,* please leave a review on Amazon. ***Your input is greatly appreciated.***

ACKNOWLEDGMENTS

My thanks and love go to my readers and helpful editors . . . Joan, Joyce, Karleen, and Marilyn, and the many classmates and instructors who helped shape this book through the Continuing Studies program at Stanford and the Writers League of Texas. Appreciation also to the team at The Cadence Group for helping me bring the first of the Brentwood Women Mysteries to the public.

My sincere thanks.

W. H. Adair

ABOUT THE AUTHOR

W. H. Adair worked in higher education PR and fundraising and was nationally recognized for both advertising campaigns and crisis communication efforts. Her first published writing was nonfiction, including *Our Time: 75 Years of the University of Houston.* Upon retirement, she completed the eighteen-month Certificate Program in Novel Writing at Stanford University. The program produced her first novel, *The Broken Hallelujah*, about a woman's quest to find her grandfather listed MIA in Vietnam fifty years ago. *The Broken Hallelujah* received outstanding reviews from both women's fiction readers and reviewers and from the Vietnam Veterans Book Review. It was awarded the 2023 Bronze Medal for wartime fiction by the Independent Publishers Book Awards, listed as a finalist in the International Book Awards, and was a finalist for historical and debut fiction and cover design from the Page Turner awards.

Deliver Us from Evil . . . and the Six O'Clock News is the first in a three-book series of Brentwood Women Mysteries, each featuring one of the Brentwood women introduced in this book. Hildy's story will be followed by a mystery involving her mother, Victoria, and unearthing a twenty-year mystery that will impact the entire family. Grace's story will also reach back to the 1920s to solve the murder of an early relative and pioneering investigative journalist.

Ms. Adair is a member of the Women's Fiction Writers Association, the Historical Fiction Writers, and the Writer's League of Texas. She lives in Houston, Texas, with her yappy white schnauzer, Jade, and her serene Russian Blue feline, Yara, who are indeed the real-life inspiration for Shasta and Catrina.

Hildy, Victoria, and Grace will return spring 2024 in a new adventure, ***Deadly as a Walk in the Park***, currently available on Amazon for preorder. To get a look at the first chapter, visit my website at www.bungalowbookspublishing.com/.

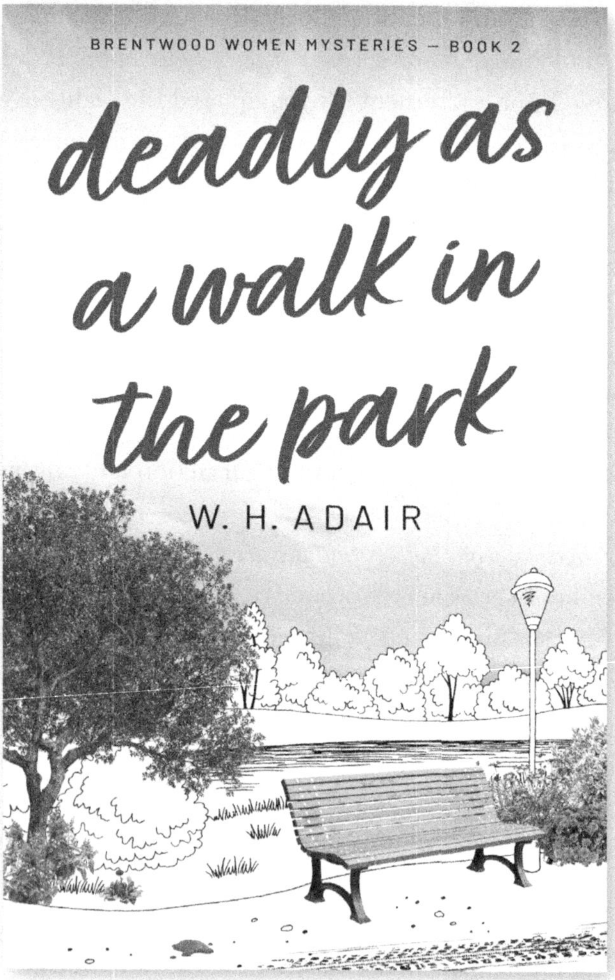

deadly as a walk in the park...

VICTORIA BRENTWOOD DELIGHTS IN her current life: a daughter, granddaughter, and soon-to-be great-granddaughter living nearby; a smooth transition from her CEO/owner's position at R&V Oil Services to board chair of the Houston Charities Foundation; a great house and neighborhood; and most significantly, great friends. One of her oldest is Cameron Mitchell—next-door neighbor, philanthropist, retired founder of Houston Financial Group, chairman of the board of Gulf State University, and most importantly, Minuit's walking buddy. Minuit is Victoria's rescue greyhound who looks forward to her daily outing with Cam.

Victoria's well-ordered world crumbles when Cam is killed. With Minuit a witness and so many connections between Cam and her family, Victoria decides to bring her inquisitive team back together to investigate his death. When she discovers a possible link to the hit-and-run death of her husband, Robert, more than twenty years before and learns of some possible unsavory transactions Robert made in the oil bust of the 1980s, Victoria is convinced that only she and her daughter, Hildegard, and granddaughter, Grace, can successfully solve Cam's murder and bring closure to Robert's twenty-two-year unsolved killing.

Hildegard signs on from her position as crisis manager for Gulf State University. A recent construction contract involving a friend of Cam Mitchell is under investigation. Grace uses her contacts at the *Dallas Morning News* to do deep background checks on the key suspects: Cameron's son and heir, Edwin, who has a gambling problem; Gerard Moulen, the intriguing owner of Golden Voodoo Casino in Lake Charles; John Canterbury, Cam's friend and owner of Canterbury Construction; and the Right Reverend Thaddeus Light of the Everlasting Journey Ministry, a surprise beneficiary in Cam's will.

Count on all three feisty furry friends to be involved: Minuit, Victoria's sleek black greyhound; Shasta, Hildy's yappy white schnauzer; and Catrina, Grace's regal Russian Blue feline.

Made in the USA
Coppell, TX
03 February 2024

28543976R20148